Good Night Sweet Ladies

Books by Caroline Blackwood

For All That I Found There
The Stepdaughter
Great Granny Webster
The Fate of Mary Rose

Good Night Sweet Ladies

CAROLINE
BLACKWOOD

Heinemann : London

William Heinemann Ltd
10 Upper Grosvenor Street, London W1X 9PA

LONDON MELBOURNE TORONTO
JOHANNESBURG AUCKLAND

First published 1983

'Taft's Wife' was first published in *The Observer*, 13 August 1978, as 'The Lunch'.

'Olga' was first published in *New Edinburgh Review*, 1983, as 'Olga's Cocktail Hour'.

ISBN 434 07465 9

Photoset in Great Britain by
Rowland Phototypesetting Ltd, Bury St Edmunds, Suffolk
and printed by St Edmundsbury Press
Bury St Edmunds, Suffolk

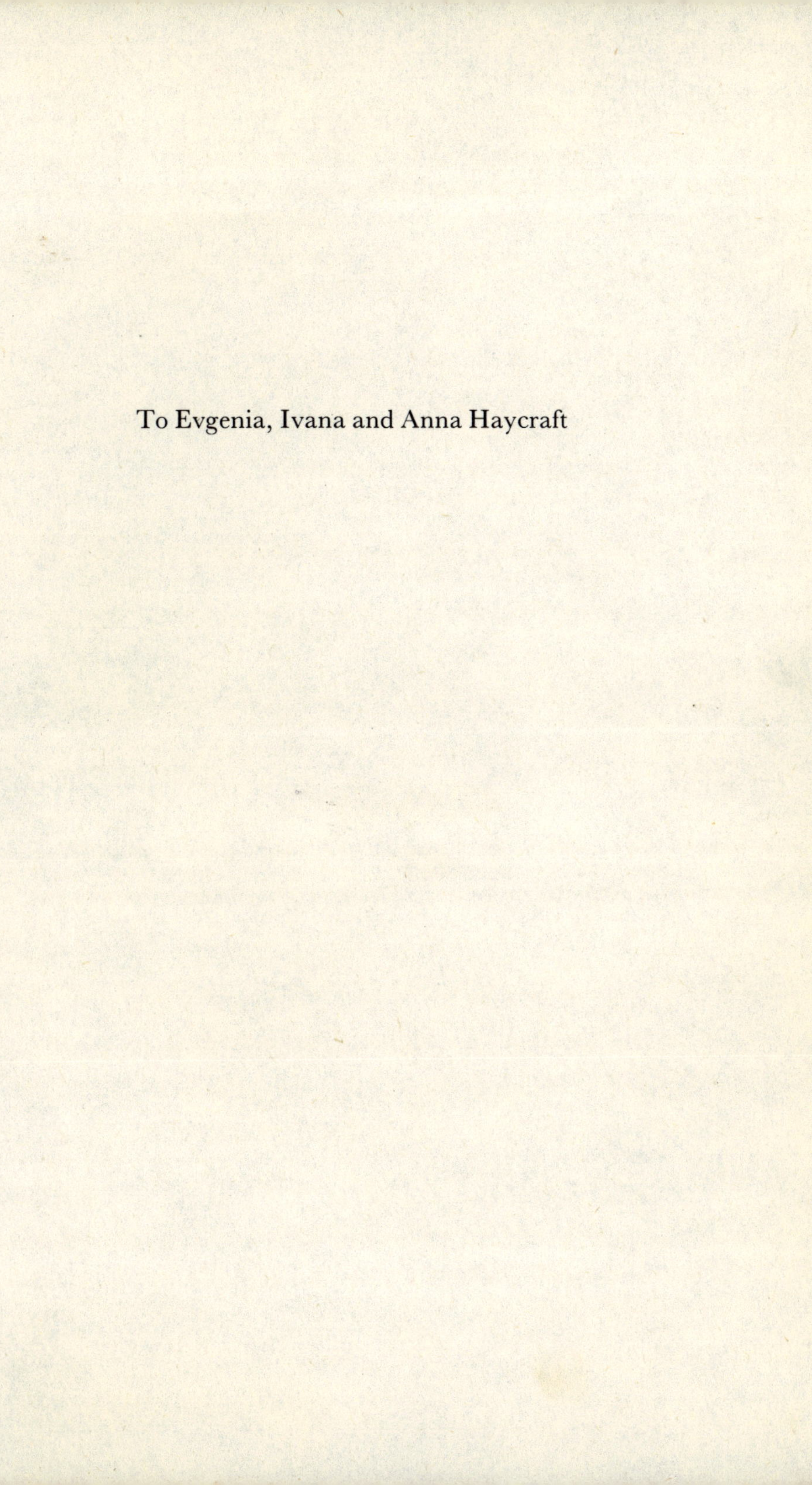

To Evgenia, Ivana and Anna Haycraft

Contents

Matron

She always liked to boast that never once in her long career had she ever made 'exceptions'. In her professional capacity she had insisted that everything be done precisely to the rule. Once one started to make 'exceptions' Matron was convinced that one invited future chaos, the last thing she saw as desirable while she was running a hospital ward.

Yet she had made a monumental 'exception' in the case of Mrs Appleseed. She admitted it to herself. She thought about it ceaselessly when she went home at night. Her own behaviour both startled and appalled her.

When Matron was off-duty she liked to review everything that had occurred while she had been on duty. A perfectionist, Matron demanded the very highest level of conduct in her hospital. She therefore submitted all her daily actions to the most ruthless of mental court-martials. Only if she was viciously self-critical did she feel entitled to behave to others with her renowned severity.

Matron had learnt how to tyrannise the hospital personnel. She had forced them to address her as 'Matron' even though the title was anachronistic. 'Matron' had a force and a resonance that she saw as hopelessly lacking in the feeble newfangled 'Sister' that was currently in usage. She was quite aware that behind her back they called her the 'Snorting Dragon' and she was proud of her nickname for she believed that, unless you inspired fear, it was impossible to assert constructive authority.

She was famous for her tantrums. A lot of her ferocity was bluff, for she believed that a capacity for pretence was essential to her calling. The fury Matron liked to display whenever she discovered a sloppiness, or a disobedience, was often hardly felt by her. Perversely, it was all the more frightening for that very reason. Her rages were given an added dramatic dimension because they stemmed from her sense of duty rather than emotion.

In the hours when Matron was off-duty she went back to her functional flatlet in Swiss Cottage and lay down on her bed. She never took off her uniform while she was resting although she was scrupulously clean in her habits and always changed into a fresh uniform twice a day. She removed her elasticated belt, and she loosened her collar. She took off her cap and placed it on the little bedside table that held her lamp and a photograph of her adored dead father wearing his military uniform. She liked to place her head-dress in front of him every night as if it was an offering.

The idea of wearing a nightgown was ridiculous to Matron. She always lay on top of her bed since she disliked the constricting sensation of lying between sheets. If it was cold in the winter, she covered herself with a blanket. She felt comfortable in her uniform for it gave her the feeling that, like a dozing sentry, she was ever ready to be on call if any emergency demanded it.

Lying flat on her back on her bed, Matron liked to drift into a half sleep while she listened to classical music. She found it pleasant to rest her feet which were always painful and swollen from her ceaseless coverage of the long corridors of the hospital. She knew little about music, but when she turned on her radio, she found it soothing after the clang and the hurly-burly of the ward.

She felt it was lucky that she was a woman who needed little sleep. If she stretched out for only a few hours, she could get up feeling just as refreshed and ready to resume work as if she had spent the whole night sleeping. But in the last few weeks her periods of relaxation had been ruined by a tormenting sense of her own unworthiness. Recently when Matron got to the end of the day she found it hard to believe that yet another night had come and still she seemed to be getting away with it – that the thing she most dreaded had still not happened – that no-one had yet accused her and made the unanswerable complaint. It couldn't go on forever like this. She saw her own lapse as much too horrifying. It was also much too public. She knew it was useless to hope that terror of her temper and her olympian air of authority would blind forever all the doctors, the nurses, and the patients, to her disgraceful aberration. They were not paralysed rabbits, too dazzled by the ferocious blaze of the headlights to see the dark silhouette of the car.

Feeling irritable and anxious lying resting on her bed, her mind whirled like the propellers of a plane as she tried to think up ways to defend her action if anyone should asked for an explanation.

For five long weeks now Matron had allowed Mrs Appleseed to eat not only breakfast and lunch but also supper sitting beside her husband's bed in the ward. Admittedly Mrs Appleseed rarely took more than a mouthful when the nurses carried these meals to her on plastic mushroom-coloured trays. But for Matron that fact was little consolation. All she could think about was the enormity of the 'exception'.

It had always been one of her most fiercely held rules that no visitors to the hospital were to be allowed to taste one single crumb of the patient's food. Once she was to allow visitors to start dropping in to have a free meal at the hospital's expense, Matron could only visualise a pattern of exploitative behaviour that would expand until the situation became a nightmare. The patients were almost invariably unhungry. Matron saw the visitors of patients as dangerously healthy, all too often young, therefore potentially very hungry indeed. If she was ever once to allow some relative to eat the hospital food that had been left untouched by a patient, then, in Matron's view, there would never be an end to it. Very soon she would have the vaguest of acquaintances dropping in to the hospital to pick up a free lunch or a supper.

To Matron, such a prospect seemed horrific. If she was to allow her ward to be treated as if it was a soup kitchen, she visualised conditions during visiting hours becoming like those in the Underground in the rush hour. All standards of hygiene would instantly drop to danger point. Her nurses would be unable to fulfil their duties for it would become impossible for them to wheel the emergency stretcher-cases through the greedy free-loading throngs.

It was this terrible hallucinatory vision which had made Matron act so harshly to the shaggy-haired young man two months ago. She happened to be making a round of the ward, when she had caught a young man with ill-cut hair eating his mother's custard. His mouth had been full of it when she came storming up behind him and surprised him.

Matron had deliberately raised her voice so that her tone resembled that of a drill-sergeant. She had felt it was immensely important that she should draw as much attention to the incident as possible. She ordered the young man to spit out the custard on a plate. She gave him warning that if he refused to do what she asked, she would make him leave the hospital immediately. She would also give instructions that never again would he be allowed to revisit his mother in the ward.

The young man had looked utterly terrified, seeing her

looming there above him, blindingly white in her uniform, with blazing blue gimlet eyes. Matron was a very tall woman. She had a particularly massive build and the muscular shoulders of a pugilist. Her victim was weedy and hollow-chested, a deprived-looking young man. Matron had not enjoyed the feeling that she was almost twice the size that he was. Rules from her school-days still had a strong influence on her, and secretly she had felt quite uncomfortable remembering the old tenet that it was unsporting to attack anyone much smaller than oneself.

She attacked him all the same. She had seen his humiliation as she forced him to cough up his yellow smear of custard while the other visitors and the patients, and various doctors stared at him with the piously horrified, yet perversely pleased, expression of children as they watch another child being smacked.

The young man went scarlet in the face. Matron had hated to see the way she had made him blush. Yet she still felt that it was urgent that he be made into an example. As Matron saw it, the young man was a thief. As a thief he therefore had to be branded.

The young man's mother was under such heavy sedation, she was unaware of her son's public disgrace. Matron had been relieved about that. Any form of emotional upset was rarely in the interests of a patient.

She had noticed that the young man seemed to be extremely attached to his mother, for he came to see her every day and he often left the ward in tears. He was clearly in an over-agitated state and with good reason, for the unfortunate woman's prognosis was extremely poor. Matron tried to take all this into account when she reviewed her treatment of him later that night. When she was alone, she was willing to view his behaviour with more leniency. Maybe when he'd taken that custard, it had been a nervous and compulsive gesture. His mother was hardly capable of saying a word to him when he visited her. For weeks he'd still loyally sat hour after hour by her bedside. There was not much for him to do in the ward. When he took his mother's food, he might have taken it in order to relieve his feeling of distress and strain. Matron suspected she had been unfair when she assumed he was trying to grab something for free. But even if the motives for his theft had not been as squalid as she originally suspected, when Matron later charged herself with unnecessary cruelty, she admitted the charge with remorse. She then decided that her cruelty had been correct. If one really cared about the future of the hospital as much as she did, the punitive action she had taken in this incident might well be criticised as excessive, yet in essence it had still been right.

Matron had lain on her bed and watched her swollen toes wriggle inside her white nylon hospital stockings, as she tried to get the circulation flowing through them. She then came to an important decision. She realised that she was not as steely hearted as she chose to appear. Secretly she would always find it upsetting when the necessity of maintaining order forced her to cause pain to the individual. But she would still continue to sacrifice the individual if by so doing she protected the interests of the many. She would always remind herself of the immeasurable future suffering which she averted every time she took any stand that prevented conditions in the hospital drifting towards anarchy.

She decided that if ever a similar situation in regard to meals recurred, she would react with exactly the same rigidity with which she had treated the young man. She would no more allow outsiders to take food that belonged to the patients than she would ever dream of allowing visitors to walk off with the hospital's towels and sheets.

When she came to a decision, she very rarely changed it. She felt contempt for those who wavered. She was an extremely able administrator, and had long ago realised that even if one had private doubts as to the wisdom of some particular policy, it was better to stick by it. Chopping and changing was fatal. People you worked with must know the exact position you held on every given issue. Once you failed to supply them with this feeling of certainty, team-work became impossible, and morale started to weaken, for no-one knew where they were.

It was her fanatical belief in the importance of making everyone know where they were, that made Matron castigate herself in private whenever she thought about the way she was favouring Mrs Appleseed. She examined her own conduct from every possible angle and found nothing to make it seem less unjust.

And from the very start Mrs Appleseed had not shown the slightest sign that she wished to be favoured. That was the thing that Matron found both intolerable and ironic. Mrs Appleseed was vaguely grateful for the gesture every time a nurse brought her a meal on a tray. But then Mrs Appleseed was one of those meek little old ladies who seemed grateful if anyone said good morning.

It was still useless to pretend that Mrs Appleseed ever had any wish to be made into an 'exception'. She never had the faintest desire to eat food that wasn't hers. She was only doing it now because someone had forced her to do so. And the person who had forced her was Matron.

Why? Why? Every time that Matron now walked through the ward she was tormented by the shocking sight of Mrs Appleseed's trays of food. Recently Matron felt it was her personal misfortune that she always passed the Appleseed's bed just when it was a meal-time. The meals started to blur in Matron's mind until breakfasts merged into suppers and she often got the impression that Mrs Appleseed was being made to partake of a round-the-clock, free banquet.

Mrs Appleseed would be sitting there silently beside

her husband whose eyes were invariably closed. Matron kept praying that Mr Appleseed would open his eyes, for then there would be a hope that all those plastic trays with their varying dishes of stodgy scrambles, their plates of mince and brussels, their bowls of melted ice-cream might seem to be intended for him. If Mr Appleseed would just occasionally open an eye, it might possibly deceive the other patients and their visitors. But even in the most unlikely event that Mr Appleseed should become quite wide awake, although outsiders might be fooled, it would never fool the nurses and the doctors. All of them knew that Mr Appleseed's nourishment was now entirely intravenous. All of them knew that it was Matron herself who had given the order that Mrs Appleseed be given three meals a day on a tray.

Nurse Sullivan had been present when Matron suffered what she could only describe to herself as her 'seizure'. Mrs Appleseed had been sitting for the last three days by her husband's bed. At night she slept in a little guest room in the hospital. There was nothing to trouble Matron about that. It was not irregular. Close relatives of patients who were not expected to last very long were often given permission to sleep in the hospital. Mrs Appleseed lived somewhere way out over the river on the other side of London. She had stated, in her mousy little way, that she longed to be there to close her husband's eyes. Mr Appleseed's eyes were shut anyway, but Matron long ago had learnt to accept that bereaved relatives tended to set great sentimental store on the idea of closing their loved ones eyelids. If Mr Appleseed was to start to fail in the night, London public transport being what it was, it would be quite impossible for the hospital to notify Mrs Appleseed and arrange for her to get to the hospital in time. Therefore Matron had given the little old lady permission to sleep in the guest room. Mrs Appleseed's round cherubic face beamed with astonishment and pleasure. 'Oh, thank you, Matron,' she had kept repeating like a child.

It was not Mrs Appleseed's free bed, it was her meals, which Matron saw as criminal. When relatives made use of the hospital's sleeping facilities, she had always insisted they provide their own food. They were made to go out to the local cafeteria – to pick up a sandwich. The way that resident relatives fed themselves was out of Matron's jurisdiction. She did not feel they should try to make it her concern. All she cared about was that they should recognise that exactly the same rules applied to them, as applied to non-resident visitors. Just because they had been granted a bed, they had no right to expect to be treated as the hospital's non-paying guests.

Mrs Appleseed had sat for three whole days and for the best part of three whole nights beside Mr Appleseed's bed, before Matron had her moment of insanity. Later when Matron tried to analyse the reasons for her own astonishing collapse of principle, she wondered if she could blame it on Mrs Appleseed's appearance. Mrs Appleseed was an old lady with an exceptionally attractive face and manner. Insofar as a woman in her early seventies can be described as lovely, Matron felt that Mrs Appleseed could be described that way. Her beauty came from a sweetness of expression, the curves of her round cheeks gave an impression of gentleness and generosity. Her eyes were still clear in a way that was rare for a woman of her age, and although she was obviously grief-stricken at the desperate condition of her husband, they expressed no bitterness. When they stared at his dying face they showed nothing but tenderness and a resignation which had dignity and calm.

Although she was an extremely busy woman, Matron always found the time to examine the conduct and appearance of all visitors who came to the ward. She felt it was important to get a personal impression of every single individual who came into her section of the hospital. Sometimes she got such an unfavourable picture that she decided their visits were detrimental to the medical progress of her patients. She then gave obscure scientific reasons to make certain they never recurred.

She had been pleased to notice that Mrs Appleseed made very little effort to talk to her husband. Matron had seen far too many upset and idiotic women who kept up a relentless patter of inconsequential conversation to patients who were in a state of near-coma. Mrs Appleseed was obviously sensible. She seemed quite aware that the effort of speaking was exhausting for the ill. On the rare occasion that Mr Appleseed's lids flickered, she always asked him the same question, but she made it clear that she only spoke to reassure him of her presence and expected no answer.

'How do you feel Harry?' Mrs Appleseed murmured.

'Poorly,' he always whispered. Mrs Appleseed then leant over and she gently stroked his limp and blue-veined hand.

From the start Matron had got a very favourable impression of Mrs Appleseed's conduct as judged within a hospital context. But innumerable other visitors had behaved with just as much good sense and decorum.

The only feeble excuse that Matron found when she thought about her own behaviour, was that at the uniquely discreditable moment when she had first made an 'exception' of Mrs Appleseed, she never could have guessed that Mr Appleseed was going to live so long. On this point she couldn't blame herself. No-one had predicted it. Certainly none of his doctors. Matron had looked at Mr Appleseed's X-rays the very same morning she had committed her act of irresponsible injustice. Hardly an organ in the poor old man's body was functioning. No-one seeing those X-rays could have suspected that Mr Appleseed was going to turn out to be one of those lingerers, one of those rare and inexplicable cases that defy the dictates of science. No-one could have foreseen that he would still be in the hospital five weeks later, that Mrs Appleseed would have been given more free meals than Matron could bear to count.

Matron had deliberately gone over to talk to Mrs Appleseed just before she gave her feckless and self-destructive permission. It was her practice to give a little warning to the relatives of patients whom she judged to be dying. Often she discovered that relatives were blindly optimistic as to the chances of the people to whom they were attached. If they were given no warning that death was imminent, Matron had learnt from experience that they reacted to it with much more hysteria and shock.

'This must be a very sad moment for you,' Matron said to Mrs Appleseed. She had judged this to be a tactful opening to an unpleasant and painful conversation. By giving Mrs Appleseed her sympathy, she was trying to make the old lady grasp that from a medical standpoint she offered her no hope.

'Oh yes . . . . It's a tragic moment for me. . . . Poor Harry . . . I never believed I would see him in a state like this.'

'Have you been married long?' Matron asked.

'Since we were both seventeen,' Mrs Appleseed whispered. 'Well, that's not quite true . . . because we courted for two years. Things went slower in those days . . . . Actually we didn't get married until we were both nineteen. You must be busy, Matron, I hope I'm not keeping you. I don't know why I'm telling you all this.'

'I imagine that you are going to miss him,' Matron found herself examining the face of Mr Appleseed as if hoping to find behind the corpse-like mask of this wheezing, dying old man, the lost features of the boy who had courted Mrs Appleseed so long ago.

'I'm certainly going to miss him, Matron. Once he goes – I sometimes wonder if I'll see much point in going on.

He's such a wonderful man. It's all because of him I've had such a wonderful life.' Mrs Appleseed spoke with sad but dignified simplicity. Just for a moment her voice quavered and then she made an obvious effort to regain her composure.

'One of us had to go first in the end,' she said. 'We always dreaded the idea of that. We used to talk about it quite a lot. I know Harry secretly hoped that he would be the first. I always secretly hoped that the first to go would be me. And we both knew it was very wrong to hope for that. We both knew it was horribly selfish.'

Matron had never been married. She had never had the slightest wish to be married. The aspirations and premises on which married couples based their lives were almost unintelligible to her. However, she could comprehend the unfortunate situation of those who were legally bound and also ill-matched more easily than that of those who considered their marriage a success. Therefore when she was confronted with people who saw their marriages as all-important, she felt so little identification with them, that as if they were creatures from a separate species, they intrigued her. Their weirdness made her find them exotic.

Could it have been something as simple and foolish as her own fascinated yet mistrustful attitude to marriage which had made her treat Mrs Appleseed in a manner so out of keeping with her most treasured beliefs? When Mrs Appleseed had been speaking about her long and loving relationship with her husband, had it seemed so confounding that she had seen it as unearthly? Had this given her a brainstorm in which she saw the old lady as a creature higher than mortal and therefore beyond all rules?

Matron never stopped asking herself these kind of nagging questions while she tried to meet the usual taxing demands that were made on her as she ran the ward. Lately while she was reading the temperature chart of a patient, she found the chart seemed to dissolve into a blaze of different colours. She knew all too well what those terrible colours were. She often now saw them in the night, even when her eyes were closed. They were the colours of all the hospital food that the nurses kept bringing to Mrs Appleseed as she sat there in the ward. As they flashed inside Matron's brain, these colours acquired all the oily and diverse brilliance of paints squeezed out onto a palette. That glutinous stretch of creamy white was Mrs Appleseed's vol-au-vent; the great splash of golden brown was her pile of chips; the patch of shocking pink was her blancmange; those cruel little rounds of emerald were her frozen peas; that haunting dab of buttercup yellow was Mrs Appleseed's margarine.

After that Matron found that all those kaleidoscopic shades would start to fade. She then saw something much worse. She saw only one colour and it looked like a vast expanse of blood. And she knew all to well what that great hideous wash of scarlet was. It was the colour of the face of the shaggy-haired young man when she had viciously reprimanded him for taking a mouthful of his mother's custard.

Matron realised that she could stop the whole thing now. There was no need to continue to torture herself. She could countermand her own order. Why not tell her nurses to stop providing Mrs Appleseed with this ceaseless round of illicit food? If this privilege without precedent were to be withdrawn from Mrs Appleseed, those horrible accusing colours might instantly recede.

It was not too late, and yet she never countermanded her order. To Matron it *seemed* too late. If she was to cut off Mrs Appleseed's food at this point, she feared it would be even more disastrous than if she was to go on allowing her to receive it. She would be drawing public attention to her original error, and she was too proud a woman to bear the humiliation. She felt that all her nurses who must already be scandalised by her permission, would be even more shocked and confused if she capriciously now withdrew it. Mrs Appleseed, because of her sweet nature, had become extremely popular with the staff. If her food was cut off, they might feel Matron was persecuting this poor old lady with her dying husband. Matron saw no way of undoing the harm she had done without doing greater damage to her own prestige. She took no action about Mrs Appleseed's food and those dreaded colours continued to flash insidiously inside her brain.

At night when she vainly tried to reconstruct her own emotions at that moment when she had first given that disastrous order, all she could remember was that, while Mrs Appleseed had been talking about her feelings for her husband, Matron had become aware of the colour of Mrs Appleseed's cheeks.

Mrs Appleseed had fluffy bright white hair and she had very rounded cheeks. As Matron examined these cheeks, she noticed that there was something troublingly wrong with them. The cheeks that went with that kind of snowy hair, surely were meant by nature to be as rosy as the apple in this old woman's name. But they were ashen as if no blood was reaching them at all. They seemed paler than those of her dying husband; they looked whiter than Mrs Appleseed's curls.

'Have you eaten, Mrs Appleseed?' Matron had suddenly asked her.

'Oh no. I couldn't eat at a time like this, Matron.'

'How long is it since you have eaten, Mrs Appleseed?' Matron's voice had acquired the drill-sergeant's tone that it automatically took on whenever she was trying to extract an answer which was hard to get. Mrs Appleseed looked bewildered and frightened.

'Oh, I don't know, Matron. Time doesn't mean much to me any more. How long have I been here in the hospital?'

'Mrs Appleseed,' Matron sounded so harsh and accusing, she might have been interrogating a suspect spy, 'you know perfectly well how long you have been here. I really don't like it when people lie to me.'

'I promise I don't quite know, Matron . . . . Everything is so wretched for me at the moment. I can only think about Harry. I feel as if I'm living in a bad dream.'

'You have been staying in this hospital for *three* whole days, and *three* whole nights, Mrs Appleseed. You have spent nearly all that time sitting here in the ward beside your husband's bed. Now that's very devoted and admirable. But I'm not concerned with that. I want to know exactly how much you have eaten in the last three days.'

Mrs Appleseed's pale cherubic face looked even more bemused and nervous.

'What have I eaten? Oh, please don't worry about that Matron. Believe me I haven't felt hungry at all.'

'I am Matron here . . . I'm afraid in my position I am forced to worry about it. You are not a young woman, Mrs Appleseed. You have been living in my hospital for three days and three nights. Am I to understand that you are now admitting to me that ever since you first arrived, you've eaten nothing at all? It's just not good enough, Mrs Appleseed!'

Mrs Appleseed's gentle blue eyes had stared up at Matron with a look of desperation. Matron's displeasure obviously petrified her. She seemed uncertain what she was expected to do.

Matron was used to bullying. Having worked since she was a girl in so many different hospitals, she had learnt that often only by a little deliberate bullying could you ever get your way. Something stubborn and unpliable in Mrs Appleseed's otherwise meek demeanour had aroused a reaction that was instinctive in Matron. She had never been able to tolerate it if her wishes were not obeyed immediately. She had always refused to listen to people when they made excuses. If she felt confident of her own rightness on any given issue, even the feeblest opposition made her hackles rise.

'Mrs Appleseed,' Matron now lowered her voice to make it sound grim and serious, 'I have allowed you to sleep in my hospital so that you could be near to your husband who is gravely ill. When I extended you this privilege, I never imagined you would abuse it. I treated you like an adult . . . . In return I expected adult behaviour. I am afraid you have disappointed me, Mrs Appleseed.'

'Oh, I'm deeply grateful for the room, Matron. You mustn't worry if I've got no appetite.'

Matron's eyes flashed with a murderous fury which was almost entirely faked.

'Well, I'm afraid you really can't stay on in this hospital unless you eat something! Nobody cares whether you feel hungry or not. Your husband is certainly an extremely ill man, but one never knows . . . . It is just possible that he might last for another week. You can't go on sitting here day after day without taking a drop of nourishment. Ever since you have been here, I don't believe that you have even drunk a cup of tea.'

'Oh, I always have a glass of water whenever I go to the lavatory, Matron.'

'I couldn't be less interested whether you always have a glass of water. You look ashen pale. You have already starved yourself for three whole days. You look really most unwell. I'm going to make one of my nurses take your blood pressure. And I'm going to insist on something else, Mrs Appleseed. I want you to listen to me carefully for I'm giving you one last warning. If you want to be allowed to continue to visit your husband in this hospital, I'm going to *insist* that you eat.'

She saw Mrs Appleseed's look of terror. There had been a clash of wills; Matron felt confident that she had won.

Her threat had obviously shaken the old lady. She felt it had been well-chosen. In this particular stubborn case it was the only one that would have worked.

'But there isn't anything to eat here, Matron.' Mrs Appleseed's voice sounded plaintive. 'Even if I didn't feel so choked up inside myself, there isn't anything in this hospital that I *could* eat.'

'Mrs Appleseed, this is absolute rubbish,' Matron said. 'Naturally the hospital can't be expected to provide food for visitors. But I'm not asking you to eat in the hospital. I'm insisting that you go out in the street. There are lots of good restaurants round here, there are cafes, there are groceries that sell food.'

'Oh, I couldn't possibly leave the hospital, Matron. Mrs Appleseed's voice was depressed and extremely low. She hardly seemed to be trying to defy Matron. She merely seemed to be stating a fact.

'I have never heard such nonsense, Mrs Appleseed. I know you are an old lady, but you still seem to be quite active. You managed to walk into this hospital ward and I see no good reason why you can't walk out of it. There are places where you can get something to eat which are right round the corner. No-one is asking you to walk any long distances.'

'I'm not afraid of the distances, Matron. But I can't possibly leave the hospital. I'd rather die than leave Harry here on his own. After all the happy years we have spent together, I'd feel like a criminal if I was sitting enjoying myself in some cafe while Harry was lying dying in this hospital. I'd never be able to forgive myself, Matron. Just think how I'd feel if I was out round the corner eating fish and chips, just at the moment that Harry's time was to suddenly come.'

Mrs Appleseed had never once broken down and cried since she arrived at the hospital. Now Matron saw that a tear was trickling down her cheek. Maybe it was the tear, maybe it was the sight of the round cheek that should have been rosy, and instead had an unearthly pallor. Maybe it was Mrs Appleseed's reference to her happy marriage, maybe it was merely Matron's overriding need to have her wishes instantly obeyed. Matron herself was never to understand why something in her mind seemed to snap.

'You are going to *eat*, Mrs Appleseed!' Matron's own voice now sounded alien to her. She felt she could hear its echo as if she was shouting in a tunnel. 'If you want to stay beside your husband until the end – you are going to do exactly what I tell you to do. And I am going to insist that you eat proper meals. My nurses are going to serve you food beside your husband's bed, so please don't dare to give me any more excuses that you wouldn't feel happy leaving him. . . . If you don't want to miss your husband's last breath, Mrs Appleseed, you are going to eat what I tell you to eat. You are going to eat three regular meals a day!'

Nurse Sullivan had received Matron's amazing order without comment. At the time Matron had been obsessed by her determination to make Mrs Appleseed do what she wanted. She therefore hardly worried about Nurse Sullivan's secret reaction to her inexplicable violation of one of the ward's most rigidly respected regulations. Later when Matron realised the horrifying implications of what she had done, she tried to avoid Nurse Sullivan as much as possible. Everytime she saw her walking towards her down a corridor, Matron darted into the nearest lavatory and stayed there until the young woman had passed. Whenever Matron came into the ward and found Nurse Sullivan giving an enema to a patient, Matron quickly left. She could not bear to meet the ginger-haired nurse's eyes.

Nurse Sullivan had always been Matron's favourite. She considered her much the ablest and most promising of all the young women working in the hospital. Nurse

Sullivan was the one that Matron saw as having exactly the right blend of qualities – the only nurse who might eventually make an excellent matron.

And what must Nurse Sullivan be thinking now? Matron repeatedly asked herself this agonising question. What must Nurse Sullivan be saying behind her back? Nurse Sullivan must be gossiping about her. Matron liked to feel she was astute when it came to knowing human nature. Not only Nurse Sullivan but all the other nurses must be gossiping about her. And not only the nurses . . . the junior resident doctors too. Even the hospital cleaners and the men who wheeled in the food trolleys. Matron kept hearing laughter in the staff-room during the tea-breaks. She knew all too well why they were laughing. Everyone in the hospital had lost respect for her.

Matron was an actress. In the public exercise of her duties, she managed to maintain an outward composure. She continued to bark out her orders with all the old ferocity. When her broad-shouldered frame came striding briskly down the hospital corridors, it still carried itself with its usual air of stern and rustling authority. Matron still knew how to wear her spotless uniform in a way that made it seem more accusingly white than anyone else's. She still knew how to carry her starched cap on her iron-grey curls as if it was a crown perched on the head of an imperious queen.

She kept all her old eye for detail. She was still just as eagle-like in detecting the smallest inefficiency. Her tantrums were, if anything, almost more ferocious than they had been in the past. They could still terrify any culprit. Her outbursts of thunderous accusatory anger were much less acted than they'd been before Mrs Appleseed's arrival in the hospital. Her fury was even more effective because it was now much more felt. It was as if the violence and explosive rage that permanently seethed somewhere deep down within the confines of Matron's psyche was only too glad to find any excuse to give itself expression. No-one seeing the way she continued to run the ward could have guessed that she no longer felt she was the same woman. No-one could have suspected that whenever she now gave an order, she secretly felt only gratitude if anyone obeyed it. Something inside Matron was broken.

She was starting to feel tired when she was on duty. Lately when she was doing her rounds of the ward, she was overcome by dizzying waves of fatigue. Never before having experienced such a sensation, she found it alarming. Recently when she looked in the bathroom mirror to see that her cap was perfectly adjusted, she noticed that her face looked nearly as grey as her cropped curls.

To make Matron's situation even more embarrassing, Mr Appleseed continued to remain alive. Mrs Appleseed continued to sleep in the hospital and she still spent her days sitting silently beside her husband's bed. Mrs Appleseed always had some tray of untouched food lying on her knee. She only ever guiltily pretended to eat it when Matron came flouncing into the ward.

Mrs Appleseed need not have been so frightened to see her. Matron no longer had the slightest intention of going near her. The very sight of Mrs Appleseed sitting there looking like a ruined shadow of the round-cheeked healthy little old lady who had first arrived at the hospital was sickening to Matron. She only wanted to keep as far away from Mrs Appleseed as possible.

Matron knew all too well that Mrs Appleseed was being extremely sly, devious and disobedient. Matron was perfectly aware that whenever her back was turned, Mrs Appleseed was being served innumerable hospital meals which she sent away untouched, hoping Matron would never notice. And Matron's trusted nurses were all colluding with Mrs Appleseed. They were removing the old lady's uneaten food and abetting her in defiance of Matron's orders. There was now the start of a total collapse of discipline and morale in her ward. The situation she most feared was beginning to occur just as she'd always known it would once one ever made 'exceptions', permitted the 'thin end of the wedge'.

She made no effort to chastise her nurses for the rebellious and flagrant way in which they were allowing Mrs Appleseed to starve herself in public. She never threatened Mrs Appleseed, made no more attempts to blackmail her. Although in other matters Matron was insistent that the medical disciplines of the ward be rigidly obeyed, in the case of Mrs Appleseed, she no longer felt in control. If she was to make public battle and force the old lady to eat, it would only spotlight the fact that Mrs Appleseed should never have been allowed hospital meals in the first place. Whether Mrs Appleseed was cowed into eating or whether she was allowed to continue her present course of open disobedience, the effect on Matron's authority was equally insidious.

Matron behaved in a way in which she had never before behaved in her entire life. In the case of Mrs Appleseed's uneaten meals, feeling too battered and conflicted to intervene, she 'turned a blind eye'. Yes, something inside Matron was broken.

Then to make Matron's position even more insufferable, Mr Appleseed was starting to make a great stir in the hospital. He was becoming increasingly famous. Matron was all too aware of the interest he was exciting, but, as the existence of both the Appleseeds was, by now, pure anathema to her, she refused to allow herself to get caught up in it.

Mr Appleseed's doctors were starting to invite other doctors from other hospitals to examine him. Totally strange grey-haired specialists were starting to stream into Matron's ward in order to take a look at Mr Appleseed, having just been shown his astounding X-rays. They left every bit as excited as Matron had feared they would be. They were unanimous in agreeing they had never seen a case quite like it. It was impossible to understand how the old man could still be alive. They said that if Mr Appleseed was to live for another week or two, he would be a case for the *Guinness Book of Records*.

Matron grew to loathe the sight of all those over-interested specialists crowding round Mr Appleseed's bed. Already she found it disturbing enough whenever she was forced to watch the regular doctors from her own hospital approaching Mr Appleseed's prostrate form. All the time they were examining the old man, she was convinced they were examining the wickedly-provided hospital food that flashed its ugly conspicuous colours from the trays which the nurses kept placing on Mrs Appleseed's knee.

Those highly-respected figures, what could they be thinking about Matron's hospital? She had always seen her hospital as an institution that was sacred, since so much of her life had been spent in trying to make it, as nearly as possible, perfect. Now, while the eyes of unknown doctors stared down at Mrs Appleseed's plates of congealing cod and frozen peas, Matron experienced such a feeling of shame and panic, it was as if the very walls of the building she had loved for so many years were starting to crumble.

Sometimes in the nights, she wondered if she would be able to go on. She despised people who refused to meet the challenge of adverse situations, but sometimes in the night she felt so over-awake, and yet also so exhausted, Matron wondered. . . .

Something new and abominable was starting to trouble her. Recently when she examined her own feelings, they filled her with disgust. The more she tried to stifle these repugnant feelings, the more they seemed to rise. How could Matron respect herself as a nurse knowing that in her heart of hearts all she hoped for now was that one of the illest of the patients under her care would hurry up and die.

Hard as Matron tried to fight it, she found that lately she prayed for Mr Appleseed's decease. Only Mr Appleseed's death could get her out of her present humiliating position. If that wheezing old man was to die, Mrs Appleseed and her disgraceful trays of food would vanish from Matron's ward. As time went by, her colleagues and subordinates might eventually forget the horrendous nature of her mistake. The importance of the whole incident might slowly start to fade.

She had always believed in the possibility of redemption in a military rather than a Christian sense. She enjoyed watching old war films about soldiers who were accused of cowardice in the face of the enemy, and then committed an act of such superhuman heroism that they regained their confiscated stripes and the respect of their fellow soldiers.

Matron's self-esteem was very badly bruised, but she could still imagine herself committing some future act of selfless devotion which would restore the confidence and respect of her staff. But she saw no possible way in which she could regain her inner self-respect while Mr Appleseed remained alive in her ward.

As the days went by and Mr Appleseed continued to breathe, Matron began to suffer from a new and secret terror that the old man's incomprehensible longevity which had already gained him such local fame soon might start to spread. She knew there was now a very real danger that he might at any moment become a medical celebrity on some vast new international scale. Doctors and specialists would then start flying over to examine him from the United States, Russia, China, the Third World . . . . The idea of this was devastating to Matron. She was certain that all those eminent foreign doctors would arrive with a preconceived and critical attitude towards the wasteful way in which the British Health Service was run. One glance at Mrs Appleseed's trays of hardly picked-at food would confirm their worse suspicions. At any moment the entire world of medicine was going to become aware of the way she had disgraced the reputation of her hospital. Sometimes in the night she felt deranged, she suffered from such acute anxiety and self-reproach. In these unhinged moments, she was convinced that the shameful situation she had allowed to develop in her ward was never going to come to an end. Mrs Appleseed would be supplied with free hospital food and sit there, disobediently wasting it for ever and ever. Mr Appleseed, who had suprised medicine already, would survive endlessly to astound it further. Matron might find she had an old man in her ward who against all odds, and by all ill-luck, would turn out to be immortal.

Matron felt such guilt about her own secret longing for Mr Appleseed's demise that she extended more care towards the old fellow than she ever before had lavished on any other dying patient. She gave orders that her two best nurses were to sit by his beside round the clock. The poor old man now had both his arms attached to feed drips and they had been dragged up high above his head, so he gave the impression that he was hanging like some old white fowl in a poultry-shop.

As a result of his long and inert stay in hospital, he was afflicted with painful bed-sores. Matron did her best to see he suffered from them as little as was possible. She gave orders that her nurses were to lift his body and dust his sheets with talcum powder every half an hour.

When Mr Appleseed finally died and Nurse Sullivan and Nurse Molloy came running down the corridors to summon her, Matron was thankful that in all honesty she could claim that she experienced not the slightest feeling of relief. She listened to the news with detachment. Its importance hardly seemed to register on her. It was as if

Matron had the premonition that, for herself, his death had come far too late.

She was standing in the corridor hissing histrionic abuse at a discomforted black trolley-man from Trinidad when Nurse Sullivan and Nurse Molloy came rushing towards her. She had just discovered that this irresponsible man had been distributing food to the patients without first washing his hands. Matron was so enraged that for a moment she found it difficult to shift her attention.

Nurse Sullivan looked extremely agitated and upset. She had become personally fond of Mr Appleseed in all the weeks she had nursed him and she identified with the distress of his wife. Normally her skin was very white and freckled, but now her face had turned such a strange purple pink, it clashed with her ginger hair.

'Matron, I think you better come at once – Mr Appleseed is starting to go.'

Matron set off with a brisk firm tread and silently followed her two nurses down the swabbed and gleaming passages. Feeling as if she was walking in a dream, she entered Mr Appleseed's ward. She went over to his bed. She took his pulse. She shook her head. She turned to Mrs Appleseed who was sitting speechless and immobile on her usual chair. Matron removed the inevitable plastic tray of uneaten food which was on her knee. She gently helped the old lady to get to her feet.

'I think you'd better come with me to the television lounge,' Matron said. 'You can lie down there on a sofa. We will bring you a cup of tea.'

Matron ordered her nurses to draw the curtain round Mr Appleseed's bed. She put an arm round Mrs Appleseed's waist, and she helped the stricken, half-fainting old lady to hobble out of the ward.

Once Matron had managed to get Mrs Appleseed to the television lounge, she tried to make her lie down on one of the shiny leatherette sofas. Mrs Appleseed refused.

'I think it's better if I keep on my feet. It's really kind of you, Matron, to take such trouble.'

'I wish there was more I could do for you, Mrs Appleseed. . . . One feels so helpless . . . . There's not much that one can say.'

Mrs Appleseed shook her head hopelessly. She looked deathly ill. Her mild blue eyes had a strange blank stare as if they were incapable of focusing. Matron was alarmed by the way the poor old creature looked. She wished Mrs Appleseed could manage to break down and cry.

'Would you like to spend the night here in the hospital?' Matron asked her. 'I'd feel much happier if you were put under sedation.'

'It's very good of you, Matron. I really prefer to go home. This hospital can only have painful associations for me at this moment. You have been much too kind already. Please don't let me keep you from your duties. I'll find my own way home.'

'Is there anyone I can send for?' Matron asked. 'I don't like the idea of you going home by yourself in the state you are in. I feel it is vital that you have some friend or relative to look after you. It would be most unwise for you to travel across London on your own.'

'I'd like to send for my daughter, Rosemary. Rosemary is working up in Leeds, Matron. She'd be glad to come down to be with me. I managed to stop her from coming to see her Dad in the hospital. I never even told her he was ill. Maybe I was wrong . . . who can tell? I didn't think it would be right for Rosemary to see her father in the ghastly state he's been in all these last weeks. It would have upset her dreadfully. And that was the last thing Harry would have wanted. I don't think it's fair to impose that kind of misery on young people. It's different for old people like me. I think I was right not to let her see him at the end. This way she'll be able to remember Harry only as he was.'

Matron asked Mrs Appleseed for her daughter's telephone number. She said she would arrange for the girl to be sent for immediately. She suggested that Mrs Appleseed remain in the hospital and rest until Rosemary arrived. She found it distressing to be with this grief-stricken old lady. She was glad to be able to send for her nearest relative. At least that was a constructive action. Although Matron longed to be able to do something to help Mrs Appleseed, it sickened her that there was nothing anyone could do.

'You stay here in the lounge while I make arrangements. I think that people often prefer to be alone at such moments. Try to relax as much as possible, Mrs Appleseed. My nurses will bring you a cup of tea.'

As Matron went walking down the passages towards the desk, she thought about Mr Appleseed and she wondered if there were any routines or procedures in his case that possibly could have been overlooked. She had great confidence in Nurse Sullivan and Nurse Molloy. She assumed that they would have already sent for a stretcher so that Mr Appleseed could be moved as soon as possible from the ward. Presumably they would have started to tidy him up, to brush his hair and put back his false teeth which had been removed in case he might choke.

Although Matron considered Nurse Sullivan and Nurse Molloy to be the most reliable of all her nurses, she had learned from painful experience that it was never wise to trust anyone to do what they were meant to, unless she was there to supervise them herself. Although she felt little anxiety that her nurses had forgotten to arrange for Mr Appleseed's stretcher, the more she thought about it, the more she realised she could not have the same one hundred per cent certainty that they had replaced his teeth.

Not feeling happy on this point, she decided to check before she made arrangements to send for the old man's daughter. She was upset by the painful session she had just had with Mrs Appleseed, and Matron was already in an irritable state as she went towards the ward. She suffered from a generalised sense of exasperation that so often, with her, culminated in a tantrum. She felt tired. She could not be everywhere, watching over everything and yet the moment she relied on the initiative of others, small but vital procedures always seemed to be neglected. She remembered the complaint of Napoleon, 'Where I am not, folly reigns.'

As she walked towards the ward, she was seething as if she had already discovered a negligence. If she was to find her nurses had omitted to replace the dentures, there was definitely going to be trouble. They were not students. She saw no excuse for them. It was her regulation that the teeth of newly-dead patients be put back in their mouths immediately. They both knew quite well why it was so important. Once you allowed *rigor mortis* to set in, the jaw bones contracted, and it was often impossible to put false teeth back.

When she thought about Mrs Appleseed sitting there in a state of frozen misery in the hospital television lounge, Matron felt mortified by the idea that her nurses had most likely forgotten about the teeth. Mrs Appleseed might easily decide she wanted to say a last goodbye to her husband. In a well-run hospital there was no reason at all why the poor old lady should not find him looking as well as possible under the circumstances. The old man's daughter would soon be travelling down from Leeds. For all that Matron knew, the girl might also decide to take one last look at her father. It was for the sake of the relatives she thought it so important that dentures be put back as soon as possible. If she was to discover that her nurses had been careless on this point, Matron knew she was going to be very angry indeed.

As Matron came into the ward, she heard one of the most horrifying sounds she had ever heard in her long nursing career. It was coming from inside the curtains which were drawn around Mr Appleseed's bed. It was the sound of shrieking, hilarious laughter.

She went rushing across the ward and tore apart the curtains with such a violence that she half-ripped them off their poles. There was Mr Appleseed looking as if he was carved out of marble lying immobile on his pillows. There were Matron's two best nurses, Nurse Sullivan and Nurse Molloy, rocking around in a fit of loud hysterical giggles beside his bed.

Matron was so shocked that for a moment she just stood there staring at them as if she was paralysed. Never in her whole life had she witnessed professional conduct quite so disgraceful. That poor old man lying there – that poor old woman sitting in a state of shock in the lounge – while two of Matron's most highly-prized nurses rolled around like a couple of idiot school-girls beside his corpse.

What could all the other patients in the ward be making of this revolting behaviour? Matron could hardly bear to think about it. How could they ever again feel that they were in good hands in a hospital which tolerated such an outrage? And what if Mrs Appleseed was suddenly to decide to come back to the ward and find Nurse Sullivan and Nurse Molloy doubled up with laughter, choking and hooting, beside her stricken husband's bed. Matron found the whole thing so appalling that she could hardly believe the incident was actually taking place in her beloved hospital.

'Nurse Sullivan, Nurse Molloy, I want you to give me an instant explanation as to what is going on here!' The thunder of her question sounded deafening to herself. Her fury seemed to rebound in menacing ripples from every white-washed wall.

'I'm really sorry, Matron . . . .' Nurse Sullivan was still laughing so hard that she found it impossible to speak. Tears of merriment were streaming down her cheeks. Her amusement set off another violent spasm of laughter from Nurse Molloy. Both nurses then went off into an even louder duet of uproarious hysterics.

'Have you both gone insane?' Matron was now screaming.

'I'm really sorry, Matron . . . .' This time it was Nurse Molloy who tried to control her laughter, so as to get enough breath to speak. 'It's hard to explain why it seems so funny. But it's Mr Appleseed's teeth. There seems to be something wrong with them. For twenty minutes now we've been trying to make them stay in his mouth. But every time we get them in, they come slipping out again and there they are lying on his lower-lip. It may not sound all that funny, but if you had seen how many times they've fallen out, you might have got a little bit hysterical yourself!'

Nurse Molloy's attempt to give an explanation was fatal for it sent her off into yet another shrill peal of giggles. This had the effect of setting off another outburst of snorting laughter from Nurse Sullivan.

Matron stood and watched them helplessly. She realised neither of her nurses could stop laughing if they tried. Her explosive fury had not had the slightest effect on them. It almost seemed to be making them behave worse. In the degraded state that these two nurses were in at the moment, the very sight of Matron, looking so huge and white and threatening with her murderous eyes, seemed to make them want to laugh even harder.

Meanwhile the whole ward was in a hubbub. Nurses and doctors were rushing in to see what was happening. For weeks Matron had suffered from a paranoid terror that everyone in the hospital was laughing at her behind her back. Now the shriek of the high-pitched titters of her young nurses made her feel that her most dreaded fantasies were turning into a reality.

Matron made a plunge towards Nurse Sullivan and she

gave her a violent and stinging slap across the face. She then turned round and did the same thing to the astonished Nurse Molloy. Both her nurses still continued to be convulsed with laughter. But now they seemed to be moaning and half-crying at the same time.

'I hope I have given you something to laugh at.' Matron hissed at them. 'I'm going to leave you now and give you a chance to pull yourselves together. I am warning you, Nurse Sullivan and Nurse Molloy, you have not heard the end of this. And unless those teeth are correctly inserted by the time I come back here – I can tell you this – it may well be the end of your nursing careers.'

She walked briskly out of the ward. She then slowed down and walked much more slowly toward the lounge for she felt it was her duty to see how the old lady was feeling and do her best to stop Mrs Appleseed from going to say a last goodbye to her husband at such a uniquely unfortunate moment in the ward.

No-one seeing Matron walking down those disinfected corridors which were hung like a second-rate art gallery with splodgy abstract canvases could have guessed that she had decided that this was the last time she would walk through the hospital in an official capacity. She was going to see that Mrs Appleseed went safely home with a nurse to wait for her daughter, Rosemary. She was going to see to it that the old fellow's teeth were reinstated. She was going to carry out all the other duties that were encumbent on her as a matron. Then at the end of the day, she was going to resign.

She knew that this decision was final. As she walked towards Mrs Appleseed, she felt much more calm than she had felt for many weeks. Knowing she would only be matron for a few more hours, even the obnoxious scene that she had just witnessed hardly ruffled her. All her anger had suddenly vanished and she now saw her situation in proportion. In this new mood of icy objectivity she could admit that she might have exaggerated the disgrace of her decision to issue food that was paid for by the British taxpayer to someone who didn't deserve it.

But even when she conceded that her original view of the importance of the whole business of Mrs Appleseed's meals might have been distorted, now she had seen what her abandonment of principle had led to, she felt that her original trepidations had been correct.

She was going to resign. No pressure from her colleagues or from the hospital board would ever weaken her decision. All her life she had demanded a perfectionist's standard of conduct both from herself and others. She therefore knew that she could never go on working in a hospital where she had lost the power to exert authority to such a shameful point that when confronted with a situation or disorder, she had found no other resource than to engage herself in a display of vulgar fisticuffs with her own subordinates. Never before in her whole life had she ever once resorted to physical violence while maintaining hospital discipline. When Matron thought about the blows she had given to Nurse Sullivan and Nurse Molloy, she felt so soiled that she was almost suicidal.

She would confess what she had done when the hospital board asked for the reasons for her resignation. She knew she'd find it unbearably humiliating to make this confession. She was still convinced it was the correct thing to do. Her horror of her own recent behaviour made her feel that she deserved to suffer. She only hoped that her honesty might in the future turn out to be beneficial to her hospital. Her conduct and the immediate resignation that had followed it, might serve as a warning example to future matrons.

She was going to tell the board everything. She was going to admit to them that she had presented the patients in her ward, many of whom were gravely ill and therefore gravely in need of total quiet, with a scene quite unprecedented in hospital history, such had been the ferocity of its noise and violence.

She would also tell them that after all the years, she had tirelessly striven for the very highest level of medical care in her hospital, she had ended up running a ward in which two of its most highly-trained nurses were incapable of replacing a patient's dentures.

Starting with her original mistaken food permission, she would describe in graphic detail the way she had allowed morale in her ward to degenerate to a point where its matron inspired so little respect that finally she had been forced to behave like a common pugilist in a public boxing-ring. Even if the authorities tried to be lenient with her, she would refuse clemency. To Matron the slaps she had given Nurse Sullivan and Nurse Molloy were unforgivable. It was as if a British officer under enemy fire was to start crazily shooting at his own troops.

When she came back into the television lounge, she found Mrs Appleseed still sitting on the shiny leatherette sofa. She had the same blank stunned expression. She hardly seemed to notice Matron's presence.

'How are you feeling, Mrs Appleseed?'

'Poorly.'

Matron noticed she used the same word that her dead husband had always used.

'I've been trying to think what would be the best thing to do for you,' Matron said. 'I've decided that you might feel better if you leave the hospital immediately. As you say, it can only have very upsetting associations for you.'

If Mrs Appleseed was despatched to her home, it would remove the pressing danger that she might go back into the ward where, for all Matron knew, any kind of abysmal situation of chaos might still be reigning and where this poor old lady might well find Nurse Molloy and Nurse Sullivan still roaring with laughter as they played the fool with her dead husband's teeth.

'One of my nurses is going to take you back to your home in a taxi, Mrs Appleseed. The fare will be paid for by the hospital.' As Matron knew she would be resigning in a few hours, she had lost her old terror of establishing dangerous precedents.

'You are obviously in a very shocked state,' Matron continued. 'It is urgent that you go home and lie down. I will contact your daughter, Rosemary, in Leeds and tell her to join you at your house. I will instruct a social worker to stay with you until she arrives.'

Mrs Appleseed nodded vaguely. She hardly seemed to care whether she stayed in the hospital, or left it. She seemed quite willing to do anything Matron wanted.

'Maybe it would be the best thing if I go home right away,' she said. 'I'll just go back into the ward for a minute, Matron. If you don't mind . . . .'

'Why do you want to go back into the ward?' Matron spoke with nervous sharpness. There was nothing that Mrs Appleseed could have suggested that Matron would have minded more.

'If you go back into the ward, Mrs Appleseed, you will only get yourself even more upset. I am very much against it indeed.'

'But I only want to go back to the ward for just one second, Matron,' Mrs Appleseed said. 'I'm not planning to stay there. I know that would make me feel much too distressed.'

Matron had the despairing feeling it was going to be just as she had feared. The old lady was going to try to say one last quick goodbye to her husband. Matron was determined to stop her. Even if Mrs Appleseed became aggrieved, she was not going to care. She was forced to refuse permission for the old lady's sake. Mrs Appleseed already looked dangerously unwell. There was no way of knowing if Nurse Sullivan and Nurse Molloy had pulled themselves together. If Mrs Appleseed was to go to the ward and find them still in the disgraceful state in which Matron had last seen them, she refused to take responsibility for the effect it might have on the poor old woman's heart. If Mrs Appleseed was to insist on her right to see her husband for the last time, she would have to come back and say her goodbye to him tomorrow when Matron would no longer have to feel responsible for what had happened because she would no longer be the matron.

'You are *not* to go back into the ward, Mrs Appleseed. You are going to take a taxi to your home. And one of my nurses is going with you.' Matron felt so insistent on this point that her voice had regained all its old bullying authority.

'But I have to go back to the ward, Matron.'

'Why do you have to go back? I can think of no good reason.'

'I have to go back because of my teeth.'

'Where did you put your teeth, Mrs Appleseed?' Matron was staring at the old lady's mouth with an expression of mesmerised horror.

'I left my teeth on the little table beside Harry's bed.'

'What on earth made you take them out?' Matron spoke with much more viciousness than she intended. She felt stunned. Why had she not noticed that Mrs Appleseed's lips were very sunken? She had thought the poor old creature looked peculiar, but attributed it to grief and shock.

'I took my teeth out when I had to eat all those awful meals, Matron. They hurt me when I bite. I always take them out if I have to eat.'

Matron told her that she would soon have her teeth back – that at present they were being sterilised. She didn't seem interested at all. Matron was very glad that she didn't have to tell her that her husband's dentures had still not been found.

As Matron went off to fetch the teeth she realised she had to make a public apology to her two young nurses. She would tell them she felt acute remorse for the way she had handled the unprecedented case of the mixed-up dentures. She could hardly congratulate Nurse Molloy and Nurse Sullivan on their recent comportment. However, she would pardon them, on the grounds of their youth and the bizarre nature of the situation with which they had been confronted. She would then go on to explain that in all honour she could not find any excuses for her own behaviour. She now recognised herself as a figure who was totally unfit to bear the responsibilities of her duties as matron. Tonight, she therefore intended to resign.

As Matron came to this never-to-be-changed decision she had the sensation that her blood was seeping from her body as though she had just slashed her wrists. When she returned to Mrs Appleseed, the old lady was wrapped in the cocoon of her own misery and she seemed unaware of the agony of Matron's state of mind. She started thanking Matron for all the kindness that Matron had shown her during her stay in the hospital. Her gratitude seemed ironic and tactless to Matron at this moment. But as she was used to acting she tried not to show that the old lady's thanks made her feel only bitterness and pain.

'All my life I'll never forget what you did for me and Harry,' Mrs Appleseed continued.

'I only did my duty,' Matron said. 'In my line of work I always felt that I was paid to be of use.'

Matron's feeling of intense melancholy was increasing by the moment. Yet her stubborn mind was still made up. When she referred to her work, she already referred to it in the past tense.

Mrs Appleseed suddenly asked her a frantic question.

'Have you ever had the feeling, Matron, that life has dealt you such a terrible blow that you can't see much point in trying to carry on?'

Matron looked at Mrs Appleseed's desperate greyish-white face. She wondered how long it would be until Mrs Appleseed followed her husband. She noticed that the poor old woman's voice was now suddenly choking in her mouth in a way that could only partially be blamed on her present lack of teeth. Matron went over and put her arm round the bereft old lady's shoulders. She could never have behaved with such spontaneity and warmth if she had not known there were only a few more hours in which she would continue to be matron.

Mrs Appleseed seemed to sense that there was something unusual in Matron's affectionate gesture, that the sympathy she was extending was much more personal and heartfelt than the routine commiseration she extended to all bereaved relatives. After all the long and painful days that she had spent in the hospital, it was the first time that Mrs Appleseed had broken down, and she suddenly started to cry.

'Cry, cry. . . .' Matron whispered. 'Have a good cry, Mrs Appleseed. Don't try to keep it back. It will probably do you good.'

As she spoke, she felt that her own empty and ruined future was merging with that of Mrs Appleseed. She saw it like a grey and polluted river flowing pointlessly into the distance towards an unenticing destination. She visualised Mrs Appleseed alone in her house once her daughter Rosemary had gone back to work in Leeds. She forsaw all the lonely functionless years that she herself would spend idling miserably in the vacuum of her Swiss Cottage flatlet.

'Cry, cry . . . .' she repeated. Then she remembered that she had not yet stopped being a matron. It was therefore still her duty to offer the old lady a support that was in some way rock-like and bracing.

'Even if you feel that you have nothing much to live for, you must try to carry on,' Matron said. 'You will find that life won't let you do anything else, Mrs Appleseed. While you are still living – carrying on – that is all that life is about.'

Taft's Wife

Mrs Arthur Ripstone finally told Taft, the social worker, that she would agree to see her son, Anthony, if he was brought to have lunch with her in one of the big West End London hotels. First she suggested the Ritz, then she decided she would prefer Claridge's.

'You understand, Mr Taft, that if I agree to this meeting I will have to insist on the utmost secrecy.'

'Absolutely.' Taft already disliked this unknown woman just from hearing the affected rasp of her voice over the telephone. She had an unpleasantly over-ladylike accent that masked some coarser, underlying accent with unmelodious results.

'I must also ask you, Mr Taft, never again to try to contact me at my home.'

'You can trust me, Mrs Ripstone. I would like to apologise for having written to you at your house. We were extremely anxious to reach you and we could think of no other way.' Taft's deep voice was soothing, studiedly avuncular. Through the years he had learnt to cultivate an ultra-comforting manner – so much of his professional life was spent trying to reassure and cajole.

As he went on speaking to Mrs Ripstone he imagined himself speaking to an obese and arrogant lady in her early fifties. In his mind he endowed her with an ugly high-bridged nose that accentuated the weakness of her chin which receded in crêpe-like wattles into a corpulent rose-pink neck encircled with expensive pearls.

He noticed that when he invented a picture of Mrs Ripstone, he made her much older than he knew for a fact she was. Only that morning Taft had looked up her age in the orphanage files. Taft deliberately imagined her as old and hideous. Mrs Ripstone's appearance might come as a shock to her son, but Taft, as the adult who was going to be present at this painful hotel meeting, wanted to be immune to any nasty surprises. He therefore prepared himself for the worst in advance.

'You appreciate, Mr Taft, that at this moment I am not speaking to you from my own house. I am talking from a call-box in my local village. I only tell you this to stress how violently I feel the need for your discretion in this whole business.'

'You can rely on my discretion, Mrs Ripstone.'

'Do I sense something sarcastic in your attitude, Mr Taft? Maybe you feel I am making an unnecessary fuss about the need for secrecy!' The lady-like voice was suddenly hissing with defensive anger.

Taft realised he would have to be more careful. The telephone was a dangerous instrument. It magnified the tiniest nuance of tone. Mrs Ripstone had not been deceived by his treacle-sweet courtesy. Her paranoia obviously had given her more sensitivity than he wished to give her credit for. Unconsciously he must have conveyed to this unknown woman some small particle of the hostility he felt for her. Unless he was more convincingly sympathetic towards her he feared she might do the thing he dreaded – she might refuse to come to the lunch.

'No doubt you see me as some kind of loose woman, Mr Taft!' Mrs Ripstone gave a hectic trill of a laugh. 'I promise you – nothing could be further from the truth. I am happily married. I have a lovely, happy home down here in Surrey. We have a swimming-pool. We have a tennis court. I have two adorable children. They are beautifully brought up . . . .'

Taft pressed the telephone receiver so hard against his ear that it hurt him. He rolled his eyes to the ceiling and his face contorted in an expression of agonised embarrassment.

'I have a *very* good marriage, Mr Taft . . . . My husband is older than me. He is a popular and respected man in the community. He is a very wonderful human being. He is a retired judge . . . .'

'Yes . . . yes . . . .' Taft knew this response must sound inadequate but could think of nothing better to say.

'Have you quite understood, Mr Taft, that my husband is totally unaware of the boy's existence?'

'I rather assumed that, Mrs Ripstone.'

'And I intend for things to stay that way?' The affected voice hissed with such aggression it reminded Taft of the sound of a steaming kettle. 'My husband – in his thinking – is an old-fashioned man, Mr Taft. He is deeply religious. The whole thing would come as a great shock to him. His heart is not strong. The past is the past. I see no reason why it should be allowed to ruin the present.'

'I assure you, Mrs Ripstone, I have not the slightest desire to create any trouble in your private life.'

'You sound as if you are blaming me, Mr Taft! But I not only have to think of my husband – I have to think of my children.'

'Of course you do, Mrs Ripstone.'

'As long as you understand that . . . . Anyway we will all meet next Sunday, Mr Taft. I think Claridge's would be as good a place to meet as any. I used to like the Ritz but lately I have found it gloomy. I think the Ritz has rather a dead feeling about it.'

'Exactly,' Taft said.

'Claridge's is so much gayer. After all we want the

meeting to be a pleasant one. Claridge's serves very nice desserts. When I bring my children up to London to visit the dentist they always try to force me to take them to Claridge's. They *so* adore the desserts.'

'Claridge's it shall be,' Taft said.

'There's one thing I must warn you, Mr Taft; you have put a lot of emotional pressure on me in order to make me agree to come to this lunch. I therefore feel you have certain responsibilities towards Anthony.'

'Responsibilities, Mrs Ripstone?'

'Responsibilities, Mr Taft. I feel it's your duty to warn the boy that he mustn't get ideas. He mustn't be allowed to think these meetings can ever become a habit.'

'I don't think Anthony expects very much from this lunch, Mrs Ripstone.' Taft was lying. He wanted to save the boy's pride. He remembered the thrilled, half-tearful expression on Anthony's face when he had been told his lost mother had been traced. Taft knew that Anthony secretly was hoping that once his unknown mother met him she would want to remove him from the Institution and take him to live with her.

'Well, goodbye, Mr Taft. I am looking forward to seeing you at Claridge's on Sunday. I've a feeling we are going to like each other!' Taft noticed that for the first time all belligerance had vanished from Mrs Ripstone's voice. It suddenly sounded both coy and flirtatious. Hearing this new note Taft shook the receiver with a violence. It was as if he was trying to shake Mrs Ripstone off the wire.

'You have a very nice voice, Mr Taft. I don't know if anyone's ever told you that!' Mrs Ripstone gave a tinkling seductive laugh. 'See you on Sunday, Mr Taft!'

'Bitch!' Taft said aloud when she had rung off. 'Bloody, fucking bitch!' He rarely swore. He went to his desk and started to write out a report on 'Battered Wives' in order to try to forget Mrs Ripstone and the umpromising lunch that he and her abandoned son were soon to have with her.

Taft's Wife

When Mrs Ripstone told Taft she liked his deep voice it was by no means the first time a woman had said that to him. The compliment was so familiar that it antagonised rather than flattered him. He reacted with much the same irritability and embarrassment when women told him that he looked like John Wayne.

Taft had always disliked John Wayne as a celluloid hero and he was bored by his films. John Wayne's swaggering and sharp-shooting myth was repugnant to him. Taft identified with losers, and although his strong, broad build and his rugged, craggy face resembled those of the actor he always felt ill at ease and demeaned when anyone told him he looked like the tough cowboy hero.

As a social worker Taft was dedicated and assured. In his dealings with the people he met through his work he was unselfish and straightforward. He became genuinely concerned with the 'cases' under his care. He identified with their problems and they found him practical, reliable, and kind.

In his private life, Taft was much less assured and he was often unreliable and devious. He knew he was attractive to women and he had become adept at warding them off. In his sexual relationships he was mistrustful and ungiving. By nature he was a solitary. He had a horror of human intimacy. Any girl who tried to get close to him aroused his terror and dislike, for he saw his emotional self-sufficiency as his strength and he felt she was trying to cripple and ensnare him. Taft was prepared to do his best to meet the varying needs of the 'cases' that were assigned to him. But he was in no way prepared to meet the needs and demands of any woman in the bruising hugger-mugger of domesticity. He had chosen to be known only as Taft – he liked the formality. He hated it if anyone called him by his first name for he resented any familiarity.

Taft lived alone in a neat one-room flat near Paddington station. In his kitchen there was one mug, one plate and one knife and fork. The deliberately sparse utensils in Taft's kitchen made a defiant display of his stand.

At night Taft often went to pubs alone, and he drank quite heavily for he liked to try and blunt the feeling of hopelessness and despair that came over him at the end of the day when his work had exposed him to a seemingly bottomless ocean of human pain, poverty, squalor and humiliation

Drinking in pubs Taft was often picked up by women and if he found them attractive he allowed them to seduce him, but he was careful to see that his love-affairs had no sequel. As a lover he merely 'obliged'. He was never the hunter. He was promiscuous not out of excessive lust but out of excessive passivity.

Taft slept with girls on the sofas of other peoples' houses – in other peoples' double-beds. In the night he got up and left them to go back to take a bath in his monastic flat. By morning it was as if the sexual experience of the night had been wiped off the slate of his consciousness like an unimportant chalk-mark.

Taft had a horror of female scenes and recriminations. The women he slept with were often encouraged and challenged by his elusiveness. Their pride was piqued by the indifference of this handsome, rugged man who treated them with avuncular protectiveness and then became without explanation suddenly so busy and unavailable they could hardly believe he was spitting them out of his life as if they were cherry stones.

Through the years Taft had learnt to devise a technique which helped spare him from the unwelcome consequences, the frantic telephone calls, the tantrums, the insults and the suicide threats to which he had often been subjected in the past as a result of his fickleness and promiscuity.

Taft had invented a wife. Every time Taft started a new sexual relationship he warned his partner that it could never become serious on his part for he still loved only his wife. Taft's imaginary wife had been killed in a car crash just a few weeks after he had married her. She had helped to disentangle him from so many relationships which he saw as a threat to the astringently lonely existence he had chosen for himself, that in a sense it was true, he did love her.

Taft had told so many different women about his wife that he now talked about this mythical and ill-fated figure with enormous natural dignity. She had become so necessary to Taft as a protection that often she seemed more important and real to him than the girls to whom he described her, and he could therefore often forget he was lying when he claimed he was incapable of recovering from her loss. Shielded from the repercussions of his promiscuity by the excuse of his fabricated bereavement, Taft felt that the dishonesty with which he treated his mistresses was justified because it helped to prevent him squandering emotional energy which he felt was better spent on his 'cases'.

The Sunday morning following his conversation with Mrs Ripstone, Taft arrived at St Michael's to pick up Anthony in order to take him to meet his unknown mother at Claridge's. He then travelled with the boy on the Underground to Oxford Street.

Sitting on the train Taft examined Anthony's face without making it obvious he was doing so. The boy looked so pale and strained and corpse-like it was as if the ordeal of meeting his mother had interfered with the natural flow of blood in his body. One of the nuns at St Michael's had whispered to Taft that Anthony had hardly eaten or slept in the last week.

Usually Anthony looked so scruffy that his appearance suggested that he got some kind of defiant satisfaction from looking memorably wild and unkempt. Today he had made a self-conscious attempt to look neat. His shaggy over-long hair was slicked down with some kind of cheap hair-oil. It looked flat and unnatural like an oily wig that had been pasted on his head with glue.

Taft saw the boy had put on his best suit – the one he wore for Church on Sundays. It was second-hand, shiny, and ill-fitting. Its trousers were too big for him and they hung in baggy folds round his legs. He was wearing a shirt and a tie and this too made Taft feel uneasy. Rarely before had he seen the boy wearing anything except grubby torn T-shirts and ragged jeans. Anthony kept fidgeting with his shirt collar as if he was trying to unfasten a noose which was choking him.

As he surreptitiously examined Anthony, Taft found himself trying to guess what impression the boy would make on his mother. Anthony was surely quite a nice-looking boy . . . . But his eyes had a dazed unfocused expression that made people feel uncomfortable. Anthony was tall and well-built for a boy of fourteen, but he moved awkwardly with a deliberate stoop that betrayed his lack of confidence.

'Are you nervous, Anthony?'

'A bit, Mr Taft.'

'You shouldn't be.' Taft spoke in his usual deep reassuring tones and he felt a disgust at the hypocrisy of his own comforting paternal manner. Why shouldn't Anthony feel nervous? Taft himself was feeling extremely agitated, though he was much too well-trained and controlled to show it. He felt that this lunch at Claridge's was going to be a catastrophe and he blamed himself for having brought it about.

Looking at Anthony's chalk-white, tormented face, Taft wondered if the whole orphanage policy in regard to the missing mothers was wrong. The staff committee at St Michael's had decided that if any of the 'unwanted' children in the orphanage expressed any wish to get to know their unknown mother, every effort should be made to find her and organise a meeting. The mothers were often hard to trace. They had married – changed their names and their life-styles. Frequently they had moved to different parts of the country. It had taken Taft a lot of time and dedicated sleuth-work to track down Mrs Ripstone.

Now having found Mrs Ripstone living in her Surrey house with her swimming-pool and her retired judge with his 'old-fashioned thinking', Taft wondered if it might not be better for Anthony if she had never been found.

But Taft couldn't be certain. Almost all the 'unwanted' children that he had worked with through the years seemed to have a longing to know what their mothers looked like. This longing was tied up with their need to establish some form of identity. Psychically they were all bruised, and they suffered from a painful feeling of confusion as to what they were and how they had come into an existence that condemned them to live in a beggar situation at the mercy of the sparse charity of an institution. Feeling themselves to be outcasts they were plagued by self-blame and hatred and it was hard to convince them they were not intrinsically undesirable.

Taft had tried to stop the term 'unwanted' from being used at St Michael's to describe the abandoned children. He felt the word had a pejorative brutality that was likely to reinforce their belief that there was something essentially wrong with them. Taft would have preferred them to be known simply as orphans. But children like Anthony, technically, were not orphans and the term 'unwanted' was still applied to him.

Taft remembered the unpleasantness of Mrs Ripstone's affected voice on the telephone. Would one meeting with the owner of that distasteful voice help cure Anthony's insecurity; were these meetings between abandoned children and abandoning mothers destructive events – rather than the valuable ones that the staff at St Michael's believed them to be? Taft felt an immense psychological fatigue. He simply didn't know.

'What do you think she will be like?' Anthony asked him.

'I'm afraid I can't tell you, Anthony. I only talked to her on the telephone.'

'Maybe I won't be like she hoped.'

'Maybe she won't be like you hoped.' Taft wondered if he should warn Anthony he had got an unsympathetic impression of his mother. He decided there was no point.

Taft had originally hoped Anthony would choose to meet his mother alone. But as the idea of lunching with her without a third party to act as a buffer clearly terrified the boy, Taft had felt it would be cruel to refuse to go.

Taft and Anthony went through the swing doors of Claridge's. The lobby was crowded with well-dressed people who were either arriving or leaving with a lot of expensive-looking luggage. Two Arabs with tired and decadent faces were making air-travel reservations at the desk. Taft glanced sideways at Anthony and he saw the boy was shaking.

She seemed to appear from nowhere. Suddenly Mrs Ripstone was shaking hands.

'You must be Mr Taft! And you must be Anthony!' She gave them such a welcoming and coquettish smile, Taft suspected it concealed a certain hysteria.

Mrs Ripstone was in her mid-thirties. She was so over-dressed for this lunch that Taft thought she looked as if she had been gift-wrapped. She was wearing a fur stole over a sleek dress that emphasised the curves of a neat little figure. Her face was small and pert and pretty and she had put such brilliant patches of rouge on her cheeks they appeared to be inflamed. Her neck and her wrists were gleaming with flashy jewellery, and on her head there was a provocative little hat with a waving feather.

Mrs Ripstone was wearing long black spiky false eyelashes which quivered and struggled when she moved her lids, like the legs of an overturned beetle.

'I'm so delighted to meet you, Mr Taft. Why don't we go into the restaurant? I'm sure we must all be starving. I've reserved us a table.'

Mrs Ripstone led the way into the restaurant. Taft noticed that she minced when she walked and she had very pretty ankles.

'Wait*a*! Wait*a*! I have a table reserved for three!' Frantically she waved a fawn-gloved hand at various indifferent-looking waiters. The more she tried to show that she was at ease and in control in this expensive international hotel, the more she seemed to have the dangerous lack of control of a driverless car that slips its brakes and goes skidding down a hill. None of the waiters seemed to want to find Mrs Ripstone's reserved table. Her grand manner and her over-stylised gestures of command had no effect on them at all.

After what seemed to Taft like an intolerable amount of commotion, complaint, and hand-waving and she had made everyone in the restaurant stare at her, Mrs Ripstone was escorted to her table by the head-waiter.

'Now what is everyone going to have!' She picked up the enormous and elaborate menu. 'They have very nice desserts here,' she said turning to Anthony. 'Do you like desserts? My children always make pigs of themselves when I bring them up to London and we all have lunch here after the dentist.'

Did she plan to say that? Taft wondered. Or in her state of confusion did it just slip out?

'Personally I'm going to start with a very strong martini. I've been rushing round London all day shopping and I'm exhausted. Won't you have a martini, Mr Taft? Surely the grown-ups are entitled to a few little rewards as the price for growing old!'

Taft agreed that he needed a martini. Looking round the restaurant with its crowded tables of cheerful chattering people who seemed to give off a smell of opulence which mingled with smells of over-rich food, Taft wondered if there could have been any more unsuitable place to have this humanly gruelling lunch.

'I recommend the hors d'oeuvres. Would you like that Anthony? I also recommend the vol-au-vent,' Mrs Ripstone said.

Anthony looked blank. Mrs Ripstone realised he didn't know what either of these dishes were and she explained in a patronising way.

'Don't you do any French at your school?' she asked.

Anthony nodded and blushed. Taft had never seen the boy look so stupid. His second-hand suit looked particularly shabby in contrast to the elegant clothes of the other people in the restaurant. Anthony's unhappy, unfocused eyes stared at his mother's face as if he was trying to memorise it.

'Anyway . . . Mr Taft says you are doing very well at school, Anthony. And I'm very pleased to hear it.' Mrs Ripstone was lying in order to be pleasant. Taft had never told her Anthony was doing well at school. Anthony was a very poor student and he found it hard to concentrate.

Taft said he would like hors d'oeuvres and vol-au-vent. It seemed the easiest. He had rarely felt less hungry. Mrs Ripstone started to show off again. She ordered herself some turbot and gave a bored-looking waiter elaborate instructions as to how she wanted it prepared.

The woman is under immense strain, Taft thought. The situation must be a difficult one for her. Shallow as she appears to be, she probably feels more guilt towards Anthony than she chooses to show, and her guilt is useless for there is no way she can make reparation to him. After this lunch she will go back to her Surrey home and try and forget him. Anthony is an unwelcome ghost from her past that she would like exorcised. She can hardly feel that his exorcism has been successful while she sees him sitting in Claridge's staring at her with his damaged-looking eyes. Feeling the boy's unvoiced accusation, she can only wrap herself ever more tightly in the cocoon of her own snobbish values in order to defend herself. Taft wondered briefly if he ought to feel sorry for this silly over-dressed woman. He longed for the lunch to be over.

Once the hors d'oeuvres arrived Mrs Ripstone once again turned to Anthony and made another self-conscious attempt to charm him. 'You seem very grown-up for your age, Anthony, I didn't expect you to be so tall and handsome!'

Mrs Ripstone gave her son an awkward and seductive look.

'Have you got a girl-friend yet, Anthony?' She let out a high and suggestive giggle, and she lowered her eyelids so that the black spikes of her eyelashes fluttered.

Anthony blushed and shook his head. He looked desperate.

'I don't believe you!' Mrs Ripstone gave her son a playful little poke. 'I bet all the girls are after you!'

'It's horrible,' Taft thought. 'She doesn't know how to relate to the boy. She feels so ill at ease that all she can do is flirt.'

'The vol-au-vent is delicious,' Taft said. He found it disgusting, but he was hoping to draw the fire of her attention to himself so she would stop tormenting her son with her unnatural badinage.

Mrs Ripstone turned to Taft with relief. She examined his handsome craggy face with approval. It was as if she had felt too agitated to notice him until that moment.

'I'm *so* glad you like it, Mr Taft.' Her eyelashes lowered in a girlish flutter. She suddenly seemed tipsy. As this difficult lunch progressed she had been ordering herself more and more martinis.

'It's such a pleasure to meet you, Mr Taft. You are a lucky boy, Anthony, to have such a charming, intelligent man as Mr Taft taking an interest in you!'

She ordered Taft and herself two more martinis and said it was time to have dessert. She suggested that Anthony should have the chocolate mousse and Taft should have the lemon soufflé. Both of them nodded feebly, and Taft felt he was behaving as if he was as stunned as the boy.

Mrs Ripstone said that she couldn't resist an éclair. She ran her hands voluptuously down her body in order to draw attention to the trimness of her pretty little figure.

'I'm going to be naughty for once,' she said. 'This is rather a special occasion!'

She turned to Taft and said she felt he must have a very interesting life. She then ordered him another martini without asking him if he wanted it. For the first time he looked her directly in the eyes and he noticed that she was examining him in an extremely predatory way through the spiky veil of her lashes.

Anthony sat there unhappily picking at his chocolate mousse. He seemed to have ceased to exist for his mother. She behaved as if she and Taft were alone.

'I had the feeling we were going to get on, Mr Taft. I liked the sound of your voice on the telephone. It's a funny thing about voices . . . they tell you so much about a person.'

The double martinis were throbbing in Taft's brain. He had a feeling of nausea and unreality.

Mrs Ripstone placed her hand on his in a proprietory and intimate way. 'I hope you are going to keep in contact with me, Mr Taft.' Her voice had become husky with sexual insinuation. He noticed her hat was a little askew. Her eyes looked bright and greedy and they never left his face. He wondered if she was a nymphomaniac.

He felt her hand tightening its grip on his hand. 'Now we have met at last we must really keep in contact. You will be hearing from me,' she gave a coy little laugh. 'I want to have news of Anthony.'

Taft felt the tremor of Mrs Ripstone's touch sending something rippling through his body like a sharp current of electricity.

'I want to ask you something, Mr Taft! Has anyone ever told you that you look like John Wayne?'

She was bound to say it. The dreaded compliment hardly irritated him. He couldn't feel it mattered. Neither did he feel it mattered that she had started slyly kicking his ankle under the table – that he was obediently kicking her back.

Pressing Mrs Ripstone's foot with his foot and looking as confident and rugged as John Wayne, Taft had rarely felt so defeated and depressed. He felt he had failed Anthony at this lunch, but even that hardly seemed to matter, for he could see no way in which anyone could have made this meeting have a more successful emotional outcome for the boy.

Taft could see by the distraught expression in Anthony's eyes that it had been a shock to realise that his mother and himself could only be forever strangers.

The boy had hoped that there would be some kind of automatic human bond between them – but it simply didn't exist. Taft could see that Anthony was disturbed by the fact that he could feel so little for this chattering little woman with the over-rouged cheeks – that Mrs Ripstone obviously felt nothing for him. If they could have felt a mutual antipathy, Taft had the idea it might have been better. It was the absence of any relationship at all between mother and son that made this lunch so tense and embarrassing.

Since his birth Anthony had been 'unwanted', whether Taft winced at the harshness of the term or learnt to tolerate it. All his life Anthony would remain 'unwanted', and Taft couldn't see there was anything anyone could do about it.

Taft continued to press Mrs Ripstone's foot under the table, though he felt not the slightest desire for her. It was as if physically he wanted to make some kind of contact with this woman because he hated to see the way that her son found it so emotionally impossible.

Taft saw the boy's future as incurably bleak. When Anthony left the comparatively kindly haven of the orphanage he would be unemployed and homeless. Without friends or relatives, with only social workers to encourage him, he would start to feel desperate in his isolation. Like so many of the 'unwanted' children that Taft had worked with in the past he would probably knock about the streets and eventually turn to petty crime. Taft had visited too many children who had been put in St Michael's and years later, with much the same friendly and cheery manner, he had visited them after they had been put in prison. He found it horrifying that they seemed condemned to spend their lives in some form of institution.

Taft pressed Mrs Ripstone's foot even harder – there was aggression in his gesture. But she didn't notice. He saw her look of triumph. She was delighted to think she had made a conquest.

She is probably an unhappy and frustrated woman, Taft thought. It's very possible that she leads a dismal life with her retired judge, who may well be too old and doddery to satisfy her. The illegitimate birth of Anthony all too likely was her tragedy. She is profoundly conventional, and she cares only for appearances. Presumably she saw her pregnancy as a catastrophic disgrace and now her whole life seems to be dedicated to regaining the respectable image she feels she lost through it.

Taft suspected that Mrs Ripstone was only making

such an overt sexual play for him because he knew about the event in her past which she most hoped to hide. Knowing he could never be impressed by the act of ultra-pure respectability she put on to deceive the old judge and her Surrey neighbours, she felt she had nothing to lose if she showed him the side of her nature her life now was spent trying to repress.

Mrs Ripstone raised her glass to Taft and gave him a toast, 'Let's drink to the most interesting man I've met in a long time!' She gave him a meaningful smile. Taft wondered if Anthony had noticed how amorously she was behaving.

If Anthony noticed he gave no sign. He just sat there looking depressed. Anthony's general predicament was so unenviable that Taft couldn't believe the boy would feel that things were made much worse for him by the fact that his mother and his social worker had chosen to carry on a pointless little flirtation.

Taft assumed this lunch must have been a harrowing occasion for the boy in the sense that it finally must have smashed any hopes that, late in life, his mother could start to provide him with the affection of which he had always been deprived. But if this lunch, for Anthony, had been a tragic event it had lacked the dignity that Taft felt should be associated with moments of human tragedy. It had been a meal of unleavened triviality – it had been nothing more than a sticky stew of flirtatious chit-chat, chocolate mousse and double martinis.

And now, pressing his foot against Mrs Ripstone's sandal, Taft knew he was debasing this ignoble lunch even further by his surreptitious show of sexuality. He found this vulgar little woman extremely unattractive. He responded to her advances only out of some kind of apathetic anger that could find no other outlet. He longed for this insufferable meal to be over. By making passes at Mrs Ripstone he felt he maintained some control over her. He also wanted to have something to do to help kill the time until the bill was paid.

'I have your telephone number, Mr Taft. I think it's best if I ring you. There might be complications if you were to ring me at my house!' He hated the slyness in her laugh. 'I think you can guess why!'

My God! She means it! Taft thought. Because he had been play-acting when he flirted with this woman he had assumed she was doing the same thing. Now he saw she was serious. She intended to see him again. He stared at her with such horror that she noticed.

'Is anything the matter, Mr Taft?'

'Yes . . . I mean, no. . . .' Like someone hallucinating Taft had started to have a horrendous vision of the future. He saw the devious Mrs Ripstone slipping quietly from her Surrey house while Judge Ripstone was taking a nap. Taft saw himself passively receiving the call she would make him from her local call-box. Her voice would be breathless with intrigue. A secret meeting in London would be arranged, and soon he would be standing on a station platform looking just as stalwart and confident as John Wayne as he stepped forward like a robot, devoid of will-power, to greet Mrs Ripstone as she alighted, mincing and over-dressed, from her train.

After that, Taft saw the lunch. The lunch would be at Claridge's and they would both drink many double martinis before they went up in the hotel lift to the double-room that Mrs Ripstone had taken for the night. . . .

'You look so peculiar, Mr Taft! Is anything the matter?'

Taft was staring at Mrs Ripstone in such a weird unseeing way that she was frightened. He was having a vision of Mrs Ripstone and himself grappling in the hotel bed. Their love-making was brief and perfunctory. Once it was over Taft saw himself lying naked beside her. He was starting to warn her that she must never expect their relationship to become deep or permanent for he would never be able to love any woman as he still loved his dead wife.

'Are you feeling unwell, Mr Taft?'

'I'm not feeling too well, Mrs Ripstone.' Taft suddenly felt sickened by the idea that many human choices – choices that were to have disastrous and long-lasting consequences – were made in a haphazard and frivolous fashion. Important decisions could be taken in much the same idle and capricious way that Taft saw the people at neighbouring tables order their courses from the menu of Claridge's. First they thought they wanted steak, then on a whim they felt they preferred to have the chicken, then at the last moment they changed again and decided to have fish.

Taft turned his head away from Mrs Ripstone. He couldn't bear to look at her. He found it too easy to see himself with her in that imaginary hotel bedroom. He was with her as a feeble victim of his own pattern of compliance rather than as a prisoner of passion. He suspected Mrs Ripstone was much stronger-willed than he was, although his square jaw looked as if it jutted with resolution.

Taft's ugly fantasy of himself in that shared bedroom was so vivid that he found himself carrying it further. As a result of that brief loveless liaison, Mrs Ripstone would become pregnant. Once again she would conceive in exactly the same unlucky careless way that she had once conceived Anthony . . . .

'I'm so sorry you don't feel well, Mr Taft. Is there anything I can do for you?'

'No. There's nothing you can do, Mrs Ripstone.' Taft said. There was nothing she could do. He felt that was the trouble with this dreary little sex-hungry woman with the feather in her hat. She couldn't even stop him carrying through his distasteful fantasy.

Taft saw the impregnated Mrs Ripstone confessing

everything to her silver-haired husband. The ancient Judge Ripstone would think of his own good name and be extremely anxious to avoid the scandal of a divorce. He would promise to forgive her if she hid abroad for nine months and agreed to place the infant at birth with some adoption service . . . .

Taft had withdrawn his foot. Under the table Mrs Ripstone's sandal groped wildly as she tried to find it. Taft had tucked his legs away so they were out of reach under his chair.

In Taft's hallucination he was no longer lunching with Mrs Ripstone and Anthony. He was in Claridge's alone and it was fourteen years later. Across the restaurant he could see Mrs Ripstone but she couldn't see him. She looked much older. Her face was raddled but her curls were still the colour of a marigold and the patches of rouge were just as brilliant on her cheeks.

Mrs Ripstone was lunching with a social worker who was many years younger than Taft. Also sitting at her table there was a teenage boy. He was ashen-pale and he had a psychotic expression. Mrs Ripstone was ordering him a chocolate mousse . . . .

Taft got to his feet in such a masterful way that he felt he must be acting exactly like John Wayne. He had stopped hallucinating. He was back with Mrs Ripstone in reality.

'Will you excuse me?' he said to her. 'I'm afraid I'm really going to have to leave. I'm feeling extremely unwell. I will take Anthony back to St Michael's and then I'm going home to lie down.'

'But this is terrible . . .,' Mrs Ripstone was stuttering, 'I hadn't realised you felt so bad.'

'I'm feeling very bad, Mrs Ripstone.' Taft's deep melodious voice had acquired the piously remorseful tone that always crept into it when his indolent sexual compliance ceased and he became ruthlessly determined to terminate a relationship that he found insufferable.

Taft's Wife

'I'm afraid I'm not myself,' Taft said. 'I'm suffering from shock. I had a tragedy last week. My wife was killed in a car crash . . . .'

Addy

Mrs Burton was in a taxi on her way to a dinner when she realised with horror that Addy, her old dog, was dying.

For some time she'd noticed that Addy was behaving strangely. It was as if she had become senile. When Mrs Burton took her out into the street for her evening walk, she now felt obliged to put her on a lead. Addy had once been traffic-trained. Mrs Burton used to be able to open the front door of her building and wait while the dog sniffed at the lamp-post and the railings and then stepped into the gutter to do what Mrs Burton called 'her business'. Addy never would have dreamt of defiling the pavement. She did her 'business' with such grace and her movements were so feminine and delicate she looked as if she was dropping a discreet curtsey. Having accomplished what was expected of her, she used to come trotting back obediently into the house.

Recently Addy's behaviour had become very peculiar whenever she was let out into the street. If any strangers passed her, she started to follow them. It upset Mrs Burton to see the way she would go limping after their shoes as if she was devoted to them. She had always been a very loving dog, but now when she trailed the heels of strangers her lovingness seemed undiscriminating and deranged.

Mrs Burton would call her name, but Addy seemed unable to recognise it. Mrs Burton had to run after the old dog and carry her back to the house otherwise she'd have followed the feet of strangers wherever they happened to take her.

Mrs Burton no longer trusted Addy's traffic-sense. She feared she might suddenly see a stranger on the other side of the street and decide she wanted to follow him. There was a danger she might step into the road without looking to the left or right and go under the wheel of a car.

Three days ago when Mrs Burton got back from work she noticed that Addy did not come bouncing and wagging to the door of her flat to greet her. She barked a welcome, but she remained sitting on her favourite sofa. Addy had very beautiful gold-brown eyes and when Mrs Burton went over and patted her, she noticed they had an imploring expression. It was as if she wished to apologise for a discourtesy.

Addy's head still looked young and it no longer matched her body. She was a border sheep-dog and she still had an aquiline aristocratic head, but with age she had lost her figure and it spread over the sofa like a fat cushion of brown fur.

Mrs Burton had decided she ought to take the old dog out for a walk. 'Come on,' she clicked her fingers at Addy whose portly body gave a helpless shudder. She seemed unable to move from the sofa.

Mrs Burton picked her up and carried her downstairs and took her into the street. When she was put down, Addy's hind-legs collapsed under her. She struggled bravely, but she was unable to take a step. If she wanted to follow strangers, she was no longer able to do so.

Mrs Burton became alarmed. What could have happened to Addy? She picked her up and carried her to the gutter and supported her and she managed to do her 'business'. She hated the look in the dog's eyes. It was too like the expression Mrs Burton's mother used to have when she had to be lifted on to the bedpan. Addy's eyes were yellow with humiliation. Once she'd carried her back up into her flat, Mrs Burton put her down on her favourite sofa. It was then that Addy had started panting.

Mrs Burton had wondered if she ought to get the vet. But she couldn't see what he could do for Addy. The dog was really now very ancient and her old age had caught up with her. From now on Addy would have to be treated like a crippled invalid. Mrs Burton brought her some water which she accepted. She offered her some dog meat which she refused. Mrs Burton felt it was all right to leave her and she went out to see a play with a woman friend. There seemed to be nothing very wrong with Addy except that she kept on panting.

When Mrs Burton returned around midnight, Addy was asleep. She looked quite peaceful. Mrs Burton went to bed, but she suffered from insomnia. She tossed around, restless and anxious. It was as if she was waiting for something unpleasant to happen and yet she wasn't quite certain what it was.

It was around three o'clock in the morning when Mrs Burton heard an odd sound from her living-room. It was the noise of violent scratching. She got up and went next door to investigate and she saw that Addy was no longer on the sofa. She had somehow managed to get down on to the floor and she had dragged herself into a corner behind an armchair.

Addy was squatting there on her collapsed haunches and with her front paws she was digging the thick wall-to-wall carpet of the living-room. She didn't stop when Mrs Burton found her doing this. Her claws continued to tear at the carpet as if she was a rabbit digging a burrow.

'Addy! What on earth are you doing!' Mrs Burton found herself speaking very sharply as if she expected an answer. Addy went on with her digging and there was a desperation in the way that her claws ripped the fluffy pile from the carpet. 'Stop it!' Mrs Burton shouted at her. 'Stop it at once, Addy! You are ruining the carpet!'

She stopped immediately. She had always been very obedient. Mrs Burton picked her up and gave her a soft little smack of disapproval. She saw the look of reproach in Addy's eyes. Mrs Burton was very aware of the softness and the vulnerability of her fat old body as she carried her back to the sofa. Once Mrs Burton had made Addy comfortable, she kissed her nose to show she had forgiven her. She noticed that it felt very dry. Addy was still panting and suddenly she gave such a loud pant it sounded like an agonised sigh. Mrs Burton patted her soothingly and left her to go back to bed.

The next day Addy seemed neither better nor worse. Mrs Burton took her out before she went to work and went through the same routine of lifting the weak old animal while she urinated.

When Mrs Burton returned in the evening, Addy was still sitting on the sofa. There seemed nothing very much the matter with her except that she still kept on quietly panting. Mrs Burton was tired and she felt a certain resentment when she had to carry her outside. Once Addy had drunk some water and refused some food, Mrs Burton put on an evening dress and went off to a dinner party. As she closed the front door behind her and left her on her own, she decided that if the dog still refused to eat in the morning, she would ask the vet to come and look at her.

It was not until she was in a taxi that Mrs Burton wondered if Addy had been trying to tell her something important. Had she refused to understand the poor animal's message because she didn't want to accept it? Could Addy be dying? Did she want Mrs Burton to know it? When she was digging the living-room carpet, had she been trying to dig her own grave? She had been trained not to cause an inconvenience or mess.

When Addy had followed strangers, had it been an act of despair? She couldn't tell Mrs Burton that she was dying. Even when she made signals that tried to convey this fact, Mrs Burton remained deaf to them. Maybe Addy had hoped that strangers could recognise that she was dying and treat her accordingly. Had she followed their heels with this blind devoted hope?

Mrs Burton knew that she ought to tell the cab-driver to turn round and take her straight back to her house. If Addy was dying, it was extremely cruel to let her die all on her own. She had always been so loving and obedient, first to Mrs Burton's daughter, Devina, and then to Mrs Burton. One of them should hold the poor old creature in her arms and give her some affection and comfort as she died. Addy was only a dog, but she deserved this human tribute.

Mrs Burton felt like a criminal, but she did not tell the driver to turn back. Mrs Fitz-James, the woman who had invited her to dine, had once been a pupil at the same school. They had once been great friends as little girls but the years had passed and their lives had gone in different directions and they had not kept in touch. Recently they'd met at a cocktail party, and Mrs Burton had been intimidated by the self-assurance with which Mrs Fitz-James met the world. She had turned into a very striking and elegant woman, but Mrs Burton disliked the way she had become both snobbish and brittle. Mrs Fitz-James was married to a wealthy London banker and she boasted about her husband as if she'd won him like a trophy. Mrs Burton remembered that Mrs Fitz-James had once won the high-jump on sports day. When she'd been handed a gold cup, she seemed unable to let go of it, but had stood there hugging it to her chest with cheeks that were pink with triumph.

When the two women met again, Mrs Fitz-James asked Mrs Burton a few condescending questions and soon made it apparent that she pitied her old school-friend for having made a mess of her life and wasted her opportunities. Her arched eyebrows had risen with sarcastic sympathy when she heard that Mrs Burton had ended up as a divorcee without sufficient alimony. She looked appalled when she heard that Mrs Burton had been forced to get a job in London in order to support herself.

Hoping to wriggle out of the uncomfortable spot-light of her old friend's condescension, Mrs Burton reminded her of a silly episode that had taken place when they were both at school. Did Mrs Fitz-James remember how they had made paper pellets and flicked them at the behind of the geography teacher, Miss Ball? Mrs Fitz-James remembered and she gave a tinkle of affected pleasure.

Miss Ball was most probably dead by now, but she had once been important to Mrs Fitz-James and Mrs Burton, and her voluminous behind was still vivid to them and they were each glad to find another human being who recalled it. It was on the strength of this frail bond that for a moment, they both drew closer to each other, and it was then that Mrs Fitz-James had asked Mrs Burton to come and dine.

The moment Mrs Burton accepted the invitation she regretted it. She suspected it had been issued out of competitiveness rather than affection. Mrs Fitz-James very probably wanted her less fortunate school-friend to be allowed a tantalising peep at the desirable life she felt she now led. Exactly as if they were still at school, Mrs Fitz-James wanted to show-off.

Now, as Mrs Burton rode on in the taxi, she realised that if she had found Mrs Fitz-James a little more congenial, she would have telephoned her and explained that she could not come to her dinner party. She knew it would be very rude if she cancelled at such short notice. If she defected, even if she explained that her dog was dying, she doubted Mrs Fitz-James would consider it an adequate excuse. The numbers at the dinner party would be made uneven. Men would have to sit next to men. Her hostess was a woman who obviously cared very much about such matters. If Mrs Burton suddenly refused the invitation, Mrs Fitz-James would be extremely annoyed. Women like Mrs Fitz-James frightened Mrs Burton. Their self-confidence and elegance and their patronising attitudes made her feel inadequate and uncouth. Mrs Burton despised herself for her cowardice, but she knew she was not going to turn back to look after Addy. She tried to persuade herself the dog was not really dying. Addy had become weak and wheezing, but she could probably go on for years in the same condition.

When Mrs Burton walked into Mrs Fitz-James's drawing-room, her hostess came swaying gracefully to greet her, holding out a beautifully manicured hand that gleamed with valuable rings. Mrs Fitz-James was looking even more handsome than when her old friend had last seen her, and her honey-coloured hair was looped around her ears and held in place by diamond clips. She was wearing a tight-fitting satin gown which showed off her supple and well-exercised figure. The very sight of her made Mrs Burton feel dumpy, middle-aged and badly dressed.

Mrs Fitz-James kissed her and was very gushing and friendly. She made a joke about Miss Ball, the geography teacher. She was trying to put Mrs Burton at her ease. But they had exhausted that subject and neither found it all that funny. Mrs Fitz-James then admired Mrs Burton's evening sandals and asked her where she had been clever enough to find them. Mrs Burton had owned them for years, but never before had she felt her shoes were quite so shabby, old-fashioned and down-at-heel.

'I'm really thrilled you could come.' Mrs Burton disliked the way Mrs Fitz-James was like an actress, word-perfect in her social lines.

A group of guests were standing round the ornate marble mantelpiece in the drawing-room. The men looked prosperous and upper-class, and they were wearing dinner-jackets.

Mrs Fitz-James introduced her to her banker husband. He looked much like all the other men in the room, but his mouth seemed just a little more cruel than theirs, and he had a slightly more supercilious and world-weary eye. When he was told that Mrs Burton had been at school with his wife, he looked surprised. 'How amusing!' he said.

There were also several women in long, glamorous dresses, but Mrs Burton hardly dared to look at them when she had to shake their hands. She was too frightened that their beauty and stylishness would make her feel even more unattractive and dreary than she'd felt when speaking to Mrs Fitz-James.

A butler brought Mrs Burton a glass of champagne. Out of nerves she drank it in one gulp and then wished she'd had the poise and the good sense to sip it.

A scarlet-faced man started to make conversation with her. He had blue, sentimental eyes and snowy-white hair with a fluffy texture as if it had been blow-dried. He told her that he was a race-horse owner and asked if she was interested in horses. She murmured that she liked horses very much, but unfortunately, she had never had much to do with them. He said that racing was a drug, but unlike most drugs it often made you quite a lot of money! Mrs Burton smiled with fake amusement. She suspected he had made this remark many times before, and, like an old comedian, he believed that well-tried jokes always worked the best.

The butler refilled Mrs Burton's glass and she took care not to drink her champagne quite so quickly as before. She told the race-horse owner that she worked in a firm which published educational books. 'That must be very interesting.' His white head nodded knowingly. Mrs Burton felt the conversation was swaying in the wind like a rope-bridge that connected different terrains.

Mrs Burton took a third glass of champagne. She wished to God she had never come. She kept thinking of Addy. Mrs Fitz-James was describing a house she was having built in Sardinia. She complained of the problems she was having getting the plumbing installed and the laziness of the local work-men.

'Have you ever been to Sardinia?' the florid race-horse owner asked her. He was valiant with his good manners. He kept trying to find the perfect topic that would stimulate her.

'No, I've never been to Sardinia.'

'I hear it is very beautiful.'

'That's what they say.'

The butler announced that dinner was ready. The table gleamed with perfectly polished silver and its mahogany shimmered in the candlelight. Mrs Burton knew from the look of Mrs Fitz-James's table that the food was going to be delicious. This made her feel unhungry.

Mrs Fitz-James placed Mrs Burton between the race-horse owner and another depressed-looking man with grey hair. When the butler filled Mrs Burton's glass with white wine, she once again gulped it down as if it was water. By now, she was feeling too drunk to care if the other guests at the table looked at her with horror, fearing she was an alcoholic.

'I'm feeling very upset tonight,' she suddenly announced to the race-horse owner. She wanted to prevent him from embarking on any meaningless general conversation. He seemed to be a boring and mindless man, but at least he could be her listener. She was angry that she had come to this deadly dinner party and she felt quite unable to find the strength to weave any more threads of social chit-chat. She would speak only about the subject that haunted her.

Her neighbour looked concerned. 'I'm very sorry to hear you are upset. What has happened?' She had already noticed he seemed to have a sentimental streak and now his watery blue eyes had become sympathetic and avuncular.

'I'm worried about my old dog. This evening I had the awful feeling that she is dying.'

'How old is your dog?' he asked her.

'In human terms she must be about eighty-eight, maybe eight-nine.'

'So she's really a very ancient lady.' Her neighbour nodded gravely.

'Yes, I'm afraid that's true. And recently she hasn't seemed at all well.'

'It's funny how attached one gets to the old things,' he said. 'I remember I was very cut up when my old Labrador died.'

The butler served Mrs Burton some creamy white soup which she looked at with a feeling of nausea. The race-horse owner leant towards her as if he was confiding a secret.

'If your dog is very old, I'm afraid she is bound to die quite soon. You will just have to accept it. When she passes on you must look on it philosophically. I'm sure your dog has had a very happy life with you. When she goes – you must comfort yourself with that.'

Mrs Burton looked at her soup and it seemed to have turned a hideous grey. She kept thinking of Addy digging the carpet. Her neighbour kept repeating that she had to be philosophical. He seemed to get a relish from saying that word, just as he was relishing the soup she couldn't eat.

Addy's life had not been as pleasant as the race-horse owner assumed. There had been a few years when she had been well-treated. That was when Devina loved her and they had lived in the country. At that time Devina was always kissing Addy. She played with her all day long and she had exercised her properly and let her run hunting rabbits in the fields.

It was as if Devina's love for Addy had been a childish disease like measles. She had caught a violent dose of it and then when she went off to boarding school, she got rid of it. Devina had once carried snap-shots of Addy in her purse. Now she carried love letters from her boy-friend. Devina was glad to see Addy on the occasions that she visited Mrs Burton. But her gladness was luke-warm. Addy no longer had any real magic for Devina. She would be sad to hear that the old dog had died. Something that had been important to her in her childhood would have perished. But Devina was at university now and all her other interests would soon smother the news of Addy's death.

After Mrs Burton was divorced, she had moved to London and got a job. She had taken Addy with her, but she had never felt she was her dog. Often she had been quite a nuisance to Mrs Burton because she needed to be let out and fed. But having known how Devina had once doted on the dog, she had thought it disloyal to get rid of her.

Mrs Burton had never been a dog-lover and she'd not been prepared to allow her life to be ruled by Addy's needs. When she went off to work, Addy had been left alone in the house all day. Mrs Burton could never muster any excitement when she was greeted by the dog when she got back home, although she knew that Addy had been moping and pining, and waiting in a frenzy of anticipation for her return. Addy's rapturous delight when she saw her come through the door irritated rather than gratified Mrs Burton. She disliked all her barking and squirming, and when she jumped up and put her front paws on her skirt, Mrs Burton had always pushed her down.

Addy's relationship with Devina had been one of

mutual passion. After Devina's father left Mrs Burton, the little girl had needed to stifle her feelings of hurt and betrayal by pouring her love on to an object she saw as perfect because it was not human. Everything about the dog had delighted Devina in that period. She loved the smell inside her ears and she claimed it was like the smell of car-seats. She refused to sleep unless Addy was tucked beside her under the bedclothes. Sometimes Devina made her lie on her back with her head propped up on pillows in a position so undog-like, Mrs Burton found it almost unkind. But Addy had seemed perfectly happy so she had not protested. Mrs Burton only made a fuss whenever she found Devina licking the dog's pink tongue because she was terrified her daughter would get some dangerous disease.

Devina used to believe that Addy could understand anything that was said to her. And when Devina spoke to her, it almost seemed to be true for she instantly obeyed the child's peculiar commands. Devina would give her a lump of sugar and order the dog not to swallow it. Addy then kept it in her mouth gazing up at Devina with an expression of slavish adoration. When the little girl told her to spit it out she immediately obeyed. After that Devina allowed her to eat the sugar lump and she squealed with delight because Addy had been so clever and abstemious. She then over-fed her with sweet biscuits to let her know how much the trick had pleased her. She would hug her and pat her until Addy got so over-excited she often seemed like a mad dog jumping around and barking as if she had been driven demented by such intense approval.

In those years, whenever anything upset Devina, her first instinct had been to run to find Addy. She clasped the dog in her arms as if she was a teddy bear and when Devina cried, she liked to bury her face in Addy's thick, reassuring fur.

Sitting at this formal and inane dinner party, Mrs Burton felt that she suddenly wanted to cry. She battled to prevent herself from doing so because her tears would be hypocritical. Very likely they would be treated with sympathy and that would make her feel all the more corrupt. If she was to cry, her neighbour would explain to the rest of the table that she was distressed because her beloved old dog was dying. It would be disgusting if she allowed all these strangers in expensive clothes to condole with her.

Addy had been used and violated by Devina and Mrs Burton. Devina had once needed Addy's love and loyalty as therapy and then she had betrayed her, for she had lost all interest in the dog once her adoration ceased to have any value for her. Addy had been too dumb to comprehend that human beings were fickle. When she was moved to the cold foster-home of Mrs Burton's ownership, she had always hopelessly tried to recreate the idyllic relationship that she had been falsely taught to accept as her due.

She had guarded Mrs Burton's flat as she should have been allowed to guard sheep. She seemed only to let herself half-sleep for, if there was any noise outside the door, she always sprang up with ears pricked in order to bark a warning. Mrs Burton suddenly remembered that she'd insisted that Addy be spayed. That was one more area where Addy had been cheated.

Although Mrs Burton had seen that she was kept alive, she now felt convinced her indifference towards the dog had been vicious. Once she'd moved from the country, she had made her lead the life of an urban prisoner. Addy had such a gregarious and friendly nature that Mrs Burton hated to think of all the hours that the poor animal had spent all alone in the flat.

'Have some croutons,' her expansive neighbour said. He was holding out some kind of china terrine. He started spooning some crisp brown squares into her soup. Mrs

Burton was suddenly feeling dizzy, but she looked down at them floating. They became soggy in front of her eyes, but for a while they kept bobbing on the surface and they all seemed like desperate, drowning creatures.

Her soup no longer seemed like soup. As if she was hallucinating, she saw it as a dangerous lake and she felt she ought to dive in and try to save the drowning croutons. But somehow something stopped her and she could only stare at them in panic and watch them as they perished.

'Are you feeling all right?' the race-horse owner asked her. He was not very sensitive, but he had noticed she was looking peculiar.

Mrs Burton found she couldn't answer him. She couldn't say she felt all right. By now only one of her croutons retained any distinct shape. The rest had sunk into the liquid. It was this last lonely crouton that Mrs Burton found the most disturbing, for at moments it seemed to be her mother, at other moments it seemed to be Addy.

Before she had died, Mrs Burton's mother had been very brave and angry sitting in her wheel-chair in the home for arthritics. She had watched television most of the day until the arthritis had gone into her lids and crippled their muscles so that she was unable to keep her eyes open. After that she had just sat in her wheel-chair, so immobile she'd seemed like a statue.

Mrs Burton had gone to read to her once a week. But her visits had never been much of a success. Invariably her mother had told her she was reading too fast or complained that she was mumbling. It had never been very long before her mother irritably ordered her to stop reading because she didn't like the book that Mrs Burton had chosen.

The food in the home for arthritics had been ill-cooked and unappetising. Mrs Burton continually sent her mother various delicacies so that the old lady could have some relief from the dreariness of the diet of the institution. When she visited, she brought smoked salmon and jars of taramasalata and pâté. But her mother always left them untouched on the table beside her wheel-chair. On one occasion she had screamed at Mrs Burton like a child. Tears started pouring down her cheeks. She had reminded her that if you couldn't take any exercise, it was impossible to work up any appetite. She had also been very annoyed by some hot-house grapes that Mrs Burton had once brought her. Her mother had refused to taste one single grape. She complained that the pips would get stuck in her teeth.

Yet Mrs Burton had always felt guilty that she had not invited her mother to come and live with her. Once her mother had become a total invalid, she still insisted she couldn't bear to be a burden on the family. If this claim had been a lie, Mrs Burton had taken it literally. She knew she could never have tolerated the presence of that critical old lady who would have sat all day long like some huge accusing statue in her household.

If she'd agreed to nurse her mother, the old woman would have become magnified by Mrs Burton until she seemed colossal. Her mother's fury at her own paralysis would have paralysed Mrs Burton. It would have prevented her from giving any love and attention to Devina, for her confidence would have shrivelled like a prune, totally withered by her inability to make any reparation for the cruel disease that had stricken the old lady.

Even when her mother was in perfect health, she had always had an intensely dissatisfied nature. Her mother's bitterness had once been diffused, but her arthritis had brought all its disparate strands together, and it had found a perfect focus. Imprisoned by her pain-ridden and crippled body, she had felt she could give full vent to all her ancient indignation, seeing it as finally justified.

Mrs Burton knew she could never have allowed her

home to be dominated by someone who sat in her wheelchair sometimes expressing her rage by stoical silences, sometimes releasing it in distressing little displays of demonic petulance. Even in her very best periods of bravery, Mrs Burton's mother would have sat with eyes closed in her daughter's household like some disturbing and vast grey monument that had been erected to commemorate the destruction of every human hope.

At the dinner party, Mrs Burton picked up her spoon and mashed her last lonely crouton until it became invisible. She was aware that her neighbour was staring at her in horror. She had squashed it with much too much violence. He was obviously shocked by her tablemanners. He thought, that like an infant, she was playing with her food.

The crouton had completely disappeared, but Mrs Burton felt freezing cold. Her neighbour found her weird, but he could not guess how restrained she was being. She would have liked to have screamed and jumped up from the table and run out of this loathsome house where ghosts had appeared in her soup and accused her of deserting them at the very moment when they'd most needed her. Mrs Burton controlled herself and she found her own control a little despicable. She felt deranged by guilts from the past and the present, but she disguised it and her need to do so seemed craven. She thought it shameful she was so frightened to arouse the disapproval of people for whom she had only scorn.

The dinner continued. More and more food was served. The courses seemed endless. Mrs Burton sat there and quietly endured this dreadful meal, imprisoned by her good manners. She picked at some duck and she dabbed her lips with her napkin in the most lady-like fashion. She did nothing further that could disturb her bovine neighbour. He chatted on to her and she kept nodding and giving him no indication that when she helped herself to a tiny portion of summer pudding she found it an agonising struggle to force herself to take even the tiniest mouthful. That evening it sickened her to taste anything that was the colour of blood.

When Mrs Fitz-James finally got up from the table after the coffee and the brandy she was followed by all the other women and she started leading them up the stairs to some bathroom where she wanted them 'to powder their noses'. The men remained in the dining-room and they continued drinking port and brandy.

And then Mrs Burton suddenly rebelled. She felt it would be insufferable to join the little feminine and perfumed cortège of Mrs Fitz-James. She refused to go up to her hostess's luxurious bedroom and sit around with all these ladies who would make her feel like a used tea-bag while they prinked and gushed and admired each others dresses, shoes and hair-styles.

No-one noticed Mrs Burton as she slipped into the hall and got her coat. She opened the front door very quietly and went out into the street. She was glad it was rude to leave without saying goodbye. She was relieved that at last she had done something impolite.

She was fortunate for she saw a taxi and hailed it. On the way back to her flat, she wondered if she had a fever. Once she got back to her building, her legs were shaking as she went upstairs. There was not a sound when she turned her key in the flat door. As she came in, she saw with horror that Addy was not on the sofa. It took Mrs Burton only a few seconds to find her. Addy had dragged herself into the corner behind the armchair very near where she'd done her digging. She was lying with her face to the wall.

Mrs Burton went over and picked her up. Addy felt heavy and rigid. Her amber eyes had gone dark. They had the sightless stare of glass eyes. There was no life in Addy's plump body and yet her fur still seemed to continue to have a life of its own. It felt soft and comforting and warm.

Mrs Burton stood very still in the centre of her flat cradling Addy. She noticed how quiet it was. She realised it would always be unpleasantly quiet in the flat now that she would be living completely on her own. She felt much less distraught than she'd felt at the dinner party. She had allowed Addy to die all alone, but it seemed futile and self-deceiving to torment herself with self-recriminations. If she had missed Mrs Fitz-James's dinner party and stayed in the flat with Addy, those few hours would have been unable to make reparation for all the days that Addy had spent locked up like a convict condemned to solitary.

Addy was released now. Addy had been too simple. She had seemed to believe that if she behaved as humans taught her, they would start to treat her as an equal, whereas they were only capable of endowing her with certain human characteristics. According to their varying self-indulgent whims they could turn her into a figure which embodied their shifting guilts and fantasies. But Addy had never managed to have any ultimate reality for the people she had been attached to. Once the veneer of their projections was stripped away, they could only see her as a dog.

Mrs Burton tightened her grip on Addy's motionless body. Through the years Addy had been a witness to so many painful moments in Mrs Burton's life. She had also been the speechless witness to many moments of happiness. Addy's relationship with Mrs Burton had lasted much longer than the latter's marriage.

Addy felt like a stuffed toy. Mrs Burton wished she could feel more regret for her death. All the wriggling life and bark had gone from Addy, but she was no longer threatened by decrepitude and pain and loneliness. Mrs Burton felt exhausted and frightened of the future. She envied Addy her stillness.

She suddenly wanted to make the dog a little gesture, and she couldn't tell whether her behaviour sprang from remorse or affection. As if she was hoping that her animal victim could help comfort her sense of desolation, she bent over and buried her face in the woolly thicket of Addy's brown fur.

Olga

'Which was the real me?' Olga suddenly asked us. I was having a drink with her son, Oliver. He desperately needed company when his mother came downstairs to have her single whisky with him in the evenings. Oliver's friends, therefore, tried to see that he was never alone with her. He said that whenever he had guests it was much easier to sustain the pretence that the cocktail hour he spent with his seventy-year-old mother was both a casual and enjoyable occasion. Guests could bring her current gossip and regale her with their doings. Olga then responded by telling them anecdotes from the past.

Oliver always scrutinised the faces of his friends while his mother was talking. The attention they gave her appeared to make him nervous. It was as if Oliver was searching for some small needle of condescension in their applause and laughter. Now that she was so ill, Oliver underrated her continued ability to amuse and enthral. In this brief period of the day when she escaped from the restricting and dismal routines that were imposed upon her by her illness, she would make a gallant effort to be entertaining. She had always been a brilliant raconteur. Once guests arrived and she had a glass in her hand, she could often seem able to throw off her sickness as if it was a cloak. These cocktail hours when she had company were only a very temporary reprieve for Olga, but it was obvious that she valued them immensely. She became like a conjuror producing magic from empty sleeves. Her stories were given an added fascination and poignancy by the shortness of the time she had to tell them. Olga had travelled all over the world and she had met many interesting people. A lot of her contemporaries were dead, but being an excellent mimic, she could make them come alive again. She recreated their dialogue, dwelt lovingly on their idiosyncrasies. She could take the dullest little incident and gild it with her humour and intensity until it seemed to acquire a glimmering significance. All her life she had done her best to transcend the humdrum and when she was talking she made small everyday events from the past and the present start to shine bright as wet beach pebbles.

It appeared that when Oliver was alone with Olga they fell into a silence that tortured him. He would then start to drink much too much and feel guilty knowing that her doctors forbade his mother to copy him, for he knew how much she longed to do so. Olga had always detested any form of discipline. She was strong-willed and pleasure-loving. Almost certainly she would have disregarded all the strictures of her medical advisers if she was not physically forced to obey them. She was no longer able to tolerate more than one glass of alcohol every day. Recently, if she exceeded this ration, she felt poisoned. She resented this very keenly. If there were no guests, Olga made her son feel that she blamed him for her deprivation. She also made it clear that he could not give her the stimulation that she got when there was company. The presence of guests could still restore Olga's old sense of animation and while she was entertaining them her craving for alcohol diminished.

Olga had been famous for her beauty. Now her disease

had drawn the flesh from her face. This showed up its perfect bones and magnified her huge violet eyes until they looked so large they seemed almost unearthly. Her eyes were very round and they still had the gaze of a little girl and the childishness of their expression was disturbing because of the unhealthy darkness of the sockets in which they were set.

Olga still cared very much about her appearance. A hairdresser came to Oliver's house every week and her hair, with its page-boy cut, was dyed a rich titian red. When she came down for her whisky in the evening, she took a lot of trouble preparing for this descent. She had always dressed with a theatricality that just skirted vulgarity. Now, when she got out of her bed after having spent a useless day in drugged half-sleep, she managed to look as if she was going off to the first night of an opera. She would put on purple and copper-coloured gowns made of velvet or some wonderful oriental material. Although she had become very weak in the last few months and could only walk extremely slowly, Olga still held herself so imperiously that she made her gowns seem like robes. It was hard to tell if she really understood how ill she was. When friends came round to the house to support her son while he tried his best to make her last evenings festive, she sometimes talked with gaiety and excitement about her plans for travel. She said that once she was better, she had decided she would go to Turkey. She'd been told there was a marvellous inexpensive hotel that faced the Bosphorus and served delicious European food. She also longed to revisit Italy. She thought it would be lovely to take a room in a *pensione* and spend next spring in Florence.

When she spoke like this none of us knew if Olga intended to discomfort. Her enthusiasm sometimes seemed like sadism. Did she feel she had the right to embarrass us because our situation was less dire than hers? Or had these fantasies become real to her, a device by which she denied reality and thereby conquered her fears?

Oliver colluded when his mother talked about her intentions to go abroad, but his expression looked strained and unnatural. His friends would follow his example. We all whipped ourselves up into a state of merry anticipation as we encouraged her pipe-dreams. We must all go to Turkey, we said in chorus. We must all take rooms in the *pensione*. . . .

The evening that Olga asked us what was the real her, I wished there were other guests present who could help her son to answer her. I noticed that every muscle in his face had become hard with tension. He started gulping his whisky as if he was trying to use it as a medicine.

She was standing by the fireplace. Recently she preferred to stand. If she sat down she had too much discomfort. She was wearing some kind of amber brocaded gown which disguised the emaciation of her body. It made her look admirably slim, like a young girl.

'Was the child, Olga, me?' she asked. 'Was the child eating porridge in the nursery the real me?'

Her huge round eyes had a look of actual bafflement. Although she had never been an actress, all her life she had behaved as if she was on the stage. She had always dominated any gathering. She knew just how to gain attention. But now when she asked this question, she didn't seem to be doing it to create an effect. It was as if she genuinely wanted an answer.

'Was the rebellious teenager the proper me?' she continued. 'Was it me when I stayed out all night dancing in night-clubs and spent the next day in bed?'

Neither Oliver or I said anything. There was nothing to stop her.

'Was the bride the me that really counted?' She went on, 'Was it the real Olga who was so proud of her wedding dress?'

'Would you like another whisky?' Oliver asked her. He seemed to have forgotten she was forbidden more than one by her doctors. She nodded. But she still went on with her questions.

'Was the young mother, the real Olga? Was it the real me who thought her infant the most exquisite and unique object on earth? Was it the real me that did all that business of bending over the cradle – all that sprinkling of talcum powder?'

Her monologue was clearly becoming insufferable to Oliver. I longed to distract her, I even wished she would talk about her travel plans. They were far less painful than all these questions.

'Was the beautiful sought-after divorcee, the real Olga?' she continued. She hardly now seemed aware of our presence. It was as if she expected to be answered by the air.

'Was it the real me who had so many lovers? Was it the real me who loved travel and the opera?'

She paused and looked frightened and bemused. She made odd groping movements with her hands. She seemed scared like a somnabulist who had been woken too roughly. 'None of them seem to connect,' she said.

'None of what connect?' My question was exceedingly dumb, but at least it broke our frightful embarrassed silence.

'None of the Olgas. I can't connect with any of them. Even the old lady who keeps slowly dying upstairs in her son's house – even she doesn't seem to be the real me. . . .'

'You mustn't exhaust yourself.' Oliver said. 'Let me help you upstairs. I think the nurse is waiting for you to have your medicine.'

'Are you two going out for dinner?' Olga asked her son. Her eyes stared out of their dark sockets with a hurt and accusing expression.

'Well, we might go out in a little while,' he mumbled

evasively. He took his mother by the arm and Olga never spoke as he escorted her up the stairs and left her with her nurse.

As she left in her amber gown, I tried to visualise her in the various roles she had mentioned; Olga the child, Olga the bride, Olga the divorcee and so on. But I could see only a forlorn old lady leaning heavily on her son's shoulder as he took her to the bed she dreaded.

'Let's get out of here for God's sake!' Oliver snapped at me when he came down having left Olga with her nurse.

'I shouldn't be here,' Oliver announced once we were sitting in a local restaurant. He then looked at me defensively as though he was trying to fend off some unvoiced criticism.

'When Olga was well, she always went out,' he said. 'When Olga was waltzing about in her heyday she never used to care if I wanted her to stay at home.'

Oliver was obviously very distressed by his mother's behaviour this evening. It seemed to have aroused old childish resentments at a moment when it was far too late for vengeance to be appropriate and bring him even the slightest satisfaction. I wished we could stop talking about her.

But Olga's absence at our table was like an invisible disturbing presence. We seemed unable to ignore her.

'What do the doctors say?' I asked.

Oliver shrugged impatiently. 'It could be weeks, it could be months.'

'There's no question that she knows?'

'Oh, Olga's probably known for quite a while. She's never been stupid. She's probably had more fun pretending she didn't know.'

I told him that I thought his mother was really very courageous and gallant in the way that she managed to appear so animated and carefree when guests came to see her.

Oliver said that this evening he'd found his mother cowardly rather than courageous. He thought she'd been taking advantage of the fact that no-one liked to tell a dying person to shut up.

'But that's what we should have said to her,' he said. 'She was being incredibly maddening and affected. It was agony for us to have to listen to her.'

As Oliver spoke he suddenly looked rather like his mother. I found this eerie for usually he seemed to have nothing in common with her. Oliver had not inherited Olga's exotic good looks. He had a pleasant gentle face with uneven features. Whereas Olga's hair was like flame, Oliver's hair and eyes were a medium brown, his colouring was as unobtrusive as his whole personality. He dressed deliberately quietly. His clothes were very well-chosen, but they were always unassuming. Oliver's nature was modest, considerate and tactful, and these qualities were reflected in the low-key autumnal shades of his shirts and suits and ties.

Whereas Olga's charm came from her longing to make every occasion special and exhilarating, Oliver's was much less obvious. He was charming because he always tried to soothe. He wanted to iron away all disturbance. Oliver had a need for good sense and balance and calm. I realised that it was only the expression in his eyes that made him look for a moment like his mother. They had the same look of bafflement and fear that I'd seen in Olga's eyes when she made those lost little groping movements with her hands.

Olga seemed to have felt frightened and confused because her life suddenly made no sense to her. Her son appeared to feel frightened because his own hostility towards her shocked him.

'I shouldn't leave her at night,' he said. 'I know I should stay with her until she gets to sleep. She manages to doze in the daytime, but around midnight she gets very wide awake. It's then that she needs me. Well, she doesn't exactly need me,' Oliver corrected himself. 'But she desperately needs someone to talk to so that she hasn't the time to think too much. But she can't talk to me. She's never been able to talk to me. So there's not much point in my staying in with her.'

He ran his hand through his hair with an agitated exasperated gesture.

'Why are you here having dinner with me tonight?' he asked me suddenly.

'I thought you wanted to get out of the house. It must be such a strain for you nursing Olga,' I said.

'But you aren't in love with me – are you?' His face twisted.

'You know quite well I'm not in love with you, Oliver. And you aren't in love with me either. You are being strange. Why are we suddenly talking about love?'

'I'm talking about it because I feel like doing so,' he said. 'And you are quite right. I am most certainly not in love with you.' Oliver made this statement so emphatically he seemed to intend it to sound aggressive.

'I can't fall in love with anyone,' he said. 'Olga has made that impossible.'

I became nervous. I disliked the turn the conversation was taking, and I started to make pellets out of my bread roll.

'How do you mean, Oliver? How can Olga have made it impossible?'

'Olga has always been such a great lover. You can't have two such figures in the same family. Through the years she has had so many blazing love affairs. In the past I was often forced to be so close to the flames of my mother's various passions that all my feelings dried out from being exposed to so much heat. Does that make sense to you?'

'It makes sense,' I said. 'But I don't believe it's true.'

Oliver hadn't touched any of the food he'd ordered. He had become very thin since Olga had become ill.

'It's true,' he said. 'And it's depressing to know one is incapable of falling in love. People might say that I'm lucky – but that's a stupid point of view. It's also not very pleasant to know that no-one will ever be able to fall in love with me.'

'Oh nonsense, Oliver,' I said. But it suddenly occurred to me that I'd never heard of any girl falling in love with him.

'I'm much too dull for anyone to fall in love with,' he said.

It upset me to hear Oliver talk like this, for usually he was so sensitive and tactful, but this evening he could see he was making me extremely uncomfortable, but he didn't seem to care.

'When you all come round in the evenings,' he said, 'I'm quite aware that you only come round because you find Olga so fascinating. I know you would all say you are friends of mine – that you come to give me support. But if my mother was a boring old wreck of a woman I don't believe you would all come so often.'

Oliver's tone was becoming increasingly belligerent. I'd never realised that there was so much anger behind the gentle and long-suffering character that he usually presented to the world.

'Olga is the talker in our family,' Oliver said. 'Olga is the one you all come to listen to. When my mother dies you won't come to see me very often. You will find me pointless without her.'

Oliver's self-pity was becoming very unattractive but I couldn't beg him to stop being so self-indulgent because he was obviously under such great stress.

'Olga always calls me "sweet, darling, Oliver",' he said. 'I'm afraid that expresses exactly how she sees me, and sometimes I think it's exactly what she has made me.'

I thought of Olga. Even now she still had so much vitality that she could often make everyone else in the room seem dim and ennervated. But her son seemed to be jealous of the energy that his friends found so attractive. It was as if he was furious because he felt she had passed none of it on to him. He couldn't forgive her for having been so colourful and full of life because it was these very qualities that had always made him feel depleted and outshone.

'I loathe having to fill the house with guests every evening,' Oliver said. 'I have to do it so that Olga won't be bored in my company. That makes me angry. I know my mother has always seen me as too dull to live with, I suppose that's fair enough. But Olga sees me as too dull to die with. That must mean she sees me as very boring indeed!'

I'd never realised that Oliver resented having to entertain for Olga. I felt sorry that he had to play the role of the good son to a mother whom he was convinced despised him. But I also felt sorry for Olga. Now she knew she was dying, she must find it very painful to be looked after by a child who hated her for the very liveliness that she was clinging to so desperately.

'I shouldn't have left Olga tonight. I shouldn't have left her alone,' Oliver said. I thought he was once again starting to feel guilty about her.

'Olga's not alone,' I said. 'Olga has her nurse.' I hoped to make him feel less guilty that he'd not stayed with her, but I misunderstood Oliver's reaction. When he said he shouldn't have left his mother this evening, he didn't seem to be feeling remorse, he seemed triumphant. He gave a laugh that disturbed me for it was cruel and hysterical.

'Oh, no, my mother is not alone!' he said. 'There are so many Olgas – or so she claims. All those different Olgas can keep her company. So I can go out as much as I like. She can't complain she's been left to die on her own . . . .'

Angelica

For the second evening running, Angelica, the retired actress, had arrived by taxi and come to loiter all alone in the Brompton Cemetery. She was a tall and flamboyant woman and she looked over life-size in her rippling and expensive fur coat. Her golden hair was piled on top of her head and it gleamed like a warrior's helmet. She was very heavily made-up and her skin glowed with the healthy peach tones of a thick and mask-like foundation. Her appearance exuded a confidence she didn't feel.

As Angelica walked through the black iron gates she once again suffered from a feeling of panic and had to struggle with a violent desire to leave. She found it ghastly, this immense London graveyard. She wondered whether there were many places on earth where it would be more depressing to spend a lonely evening than in these sealed-off city acres where the rain was drizzling down on the dead who were all lying there so hugger-mugger under their hideous and diversified stones.

The overcrowding in this cemetery was very shocking to her. She tried to see the congestion as comic. But she found it grim rather than amusing. She was disturbed by the way all the graves and crosses and mausoleums were so closely packed that they looked as if they were all part of one vast greyish white mosaic.

As Angelica set off towards the centre of the cemetery she felt she was in a place of remembrance that made the whole concept seem like a fantasy. Most of the inmates in this ill-tended and overpopulated cemetery seemed extremely forgotten. They had been squeezed in here and labelled with pious phrases and their dates, but they still seemed so forgotten they might as well never have existed.

Angelica felt that this was a spot which questioned the whole essentialness of existence. This was a place that demanded feelings of melancholy just as it demanded wreaths of flowers. But as she went winding through its maze-like paths and smelt once again the musty stench of desolation that rose from all these urban graves that seemed to stretch out to infinity around her, she was certain she had made the right decision in coming here. For she felt less depressed while she was wandering about amongst all these neglected mounds and these phalanxes of tilting crosses, than she ever felt in Dr Abelman's office where she went every morning to have treatment for her depression.

She wondered what Dr Abelman would say if she told him she found visits to Brompton Cemetery much more therapeutic than his treatment. She felt that it was unlikely that he would be very thrilled to hear that she'd come back for the second time to this dismal burial ground. He wouldn't be pleased to be told that one of his patients liked to hang around in this gruesome spot without having even the remotest link with any of the dead. It might be difficult for him to accept that it was very healthy behaviour. She didn't think he would be able to boast that it was much of an advertisement for his therapy.

Angelica felt rather gratified by the idea that young Dr Abelman would disapprove of her presence in the cemetery. She often felt a very deep dislike for him, finding him smug and humourless and dogmatic. However, she concealed these feelings and she was uncharacteristically meek and subdued while she was with him. When she went to his office seeking pills and sympathy for her depression she sometimes thought she must seem like a pathetic old whining beggar holding out her bowl.

'We must try to find out why you react so violently to any rejection,' he kept saying to her. 'You must try to see your depression is really anger. You are angry that Jason has left you. We must examine the way that your relationship with that young man was destroyed by your insecurity and jealousy.'

Dr Abelman believed there was a point in speaking to her with a certain brutality. He thought she could have a happy and productive future if she would only allow him to change her. He felt that once she gained some insight into the patterns of her past behaviour she could learn by her mistakes. But Angelica, who felt so fierce and defeated and futureless, only found herself more and more depressed every moment that she listened to him. She had little faith in the effectiveness of his therapy, and often the naivety of his suggestions seemed so exasperating it made her want to scream.

'I would like you to have a much fuller social life than you do at present,' he kept telling her. 'You would feel better if you went out much more and attended the opera and the theatre. You should try to mix with people of your own age. Your attachment to this young man was clearly a very neurotic one. You should try to strike up some new acquaintances with whom you can have an interesting and lively exchange of ideas, establish mature and valuable relationships.'

Dr Abelman longed for her to have 'lively exchanges of ideas', and Angelica always felt bemused whenever he mentioned this strange ambition. She wondered where he had got it from. Such exchanges seemed so pathetic and futile as an aspiration.

Angelica always found it useless to try and make Dr

Abelman understand how much she had disliked the parties she had gone to lately, for she'd seemed to spend them sitting with a whisky on some sofa and staring with disgust at the ears of the other guests.

She'd wonder why they were not ashamed to go on laughing and chattering to each other in such a confident and mindless fashion when all the time they had these absurd rubbery appendages clamped to the sides of their heads.

She dreaded it whenever any of them came over and tried to speak to her, for she felt she couldn't bear to talk to them unless they first removed their odious ears. The young men seemed quite as insensitive as the old ones, expecting her to enjoy making conversation while they made no effort to prevent her from seeing the repulsive hanging skinflaps of their lobes. The women also repelled her, for though they had various elaborate hair-styles, she could still see the sickening bulge of their ears showing through their curls. Sometimes she found the women were almost worse than the men, for she felt there was something deceitful in the way they seemed to be trying to hide the pink deformities that sprouted out like fungi from both sides of their faces by draping them with coils of silky hair.

When Angelica went out to parties, it was the enormous variety in design of the ears of the people that she met that she found so revolting, much more revolting than if they'd all had one uniform brand. She loathed the way that some of their ears were multicoloured with inner-rims and outer-rims of different shapes and shades that ranged from violet to raspberry – from off-white to bluish-black.

'Is anything the matter, Angelica?' It was never very long before someone asked her this question.

'No. This evening I'm afraid I suddenly don't feel very well at all.'

Angelica would have just caught sight of the ears of a couple of homosexuals, noticing that the older one had ears which were a pale tomato cream and inlaid with a jewelled cluster of navy blue spots. The younger one had yellow wax ears which were flecked like a bird's egg, with tiny freckles of coffee brown.

'You really do look quite pale and ill, Angelica. Perhaps you would like us to get you a taxi to take you home.'

'It's been such a lovely party, but I think I must be coming down with some little virus. It would be very kind if you could get me a taxi.'

She would have just caught sight of a distinguished white-haired politician and noticed with a feeling of nausea and despair that he had the most terrible orange plastic hearing-aid stuck deep in the disgusting hole of his raw-meat coloured ear.

'Ears obviously must have some special significance for you,' Dr Abelman kept suggesting with his customary owlish solemnity.

'Oh no. I don't think ears mean very much to me at all.' Angelica was invariably very stubborn on this point, as she kept trying not to examine Dr Abelman's baroque-looking ears with their curlicue arches and their dark inner courtyards of hair-tufted skin.

She could have easily explained why the ears of every person that she had met in the last few months filled her with revulsion. But she had never felt there was any point in trying to explain anything she saw as important to Dr Abelman. He was far too unimaginative and his literal mind had such very great difficulty in following any fanciful flights. As Angelica found him deeply unsympathetic and difficult to speak to, she often wondered if it was not rather pointless paying so much to come every morning to talk to him.

She could have explained to almost anyone in the world except this bespectacled young doctor that ever since Jason had left her, although she hated being alone, she disliked people coming to her house almost as much as she disliked going to other people's houses to be entertained. She now loathed being with friends almost as much as she loathed being with crowds of strangers. She only became obsessed by the ugliness and absurdity of the ears of other human beings because it made them all seem so very flawed. But their true flaw, only symbolised by their ears, was that they were all quite incapable of distracting her.

Recently she had found that both men and women were equally incapable of pleasing and amusing her. Even when they were generous, sympathetic and flattering they still aroused her anger. They seemed to prattle incessantly. When they invited her to restaurants and parties she accepted gratefully and her smile was false and gracious, but her eyes were fixed with fury and horror on their ears.

The whole time that she listened to them flirting and gossiping, and speaking of their careers, their money difficulties, their love affairs, she found that their distressingly visible ears made them all seem so unattractive that they seemed indistinguishable.

She tried to pay attention while they discussed current political events, the books they had read, the films they had seen, the taxes they were being forced to pay. When they talked they bored her so much that she found it hard to believe that it was not their deliberate intention to do so.

Lately her feeling of generalised free-floating boredom had become so sharp that she often felt that it was drilling through her like an instrument of torture. She was often frightened by the way that her interests had become so shrunken that they seemed to be incapable of focusing on anything except her own menacing moods. All her energies were now devoted to trying to placate them.

In recent weeks, whenever Angelica left her house and went out to attend any social occasion, it was only in the hope of improving her own moods. She felt obliged to treat them as if they were sickly and demanding invalids who might conceivably benefit from a little fresh air.

But once she found herself surrounded by people who were laughing and drinking and joking she was invariably disappointed. She only wished that she had stayed at home drinking whisky alone in her bed.

Her moods tended to deteriorate and become fouler and more petulant in the very pleasant circumstances where she had hoped they might improve. Sitting, unhungry, at dinner parties she would stare at all the expensive foods that seemed to flow on and off her plate in great tidal waves of courses. She viewed her fellow guests with a paranoid rage and horror. She felt certain that she had only been invited because she was generally considered to be pitiable. Whenever anyone tried to speak to her she suspected that they were only making an effort to be kind to her because they realised she was lonely and humiliated. She found their kindness as distasteful as all the rich sauces that smothered the fish and the meat that her hostess kept trying to feed to her. Neither friendliness nor hospitality could cheer her. All the while she was receiving it Angelica never stopped feeling that now Jason had grown tired of her she only wished that she was dead.

But she didn't feel that for one single moment when she was drifting around all by herself in Brompton Cemetery. Once she was surrounded by the deceased nothing in their situation seemed at all enviable. All her self-dramatising sentiments seemed contemptible and she realised they were completely bogus. When Angelica was all alone in the huge and creepy burial ground, the dead called her bluff.

Lately whenever she had telephoned her daughter, Susan, she had laid great emphasis on her desparing state of mind. 'I have reached a point of unhappiness, darling, when I wonder if I can really go on.'

However, she had just discovered that when she was alone with all these hordes of unweeded people in Brompton Cemetery their mass indifference to her wretchedness was more cheering than her daughter's automatic solicitude. Their indifference was so total that it became contagious and while she was with them she felt temporarily forced to share it.

And there was another reason why Angelica's depression lifted the moment she came into the cemetery. As she walked through its sombre gates all her self-pity instantly vanished. She recognised it to be such an unsuitable emotion that it seemed to go immediately underground, like the bones of all the inmates.

'Lately I feel that I am becoming more and more like those stiff and pointless female figures that you sometimes see in bad, nineteenth-century oil paintings,' Angelica had told Susan very recently. 'Day after day as I sit here alone in the elegant interior of my expensive London house I feel so unreal that I start to think that some unknown artist has only put me here in order to balance the strip of sunlight on my Wilton carpet, to make some kind of subtle colour contrast with the blackness of my own stupid piano. I begin to think that, like those wretched painted women, every fold in the beautiful material of my dress is now far more interesting than the wrinkles on my face. It's very demoralising to be forced to realise that you have got to a point in life when even your clothes and your furniture have far more interest and function than you do. You start to hope that the unknown artist will suddenly decide that the composition would be just as good without you – that he will soon take some tuft of cotton-wool soaked in turpentine and just wipe you out.'

Angelica had seen the nervous concern on her daughter's face. As she burdened Susan with her dissatisfactions she had got an ignoble pleasure from her knowledge that she could always ruin the unlucky girl's peace of mind. Susan's vulnerability in relation to her mother aroused Angelica's sadism. She was ruthless in the way she liked to make her daughter worry about her. She found Susan kind and reliable, but she also found her distressingly ordinary. Angelica always wished she could like her only child more than she did. Susan's lack of worldliness and ambition appalled her. The sight of her daughter's healthy and humdrum face always startled her. She saw it as sad and disturbing. She felt baffled as to how she had ever produced it. She found it indistinguishable from the robust, pleasant faces of all the hundreds of young married women who were to be seen pushing their baby-strollers and lugging their string bags of groceries through all the supermarkets of every sleepy country town in England.

Angelica saw Susan's life as so dismally lacking in drama that she often managed to convince herself that she was doing her daughter a favour by force-feeding her with her own surplus. Lately she had started to telephone Susan incessantly. Angelica would drink whisky alone in her bed at night and then with her mind boiling with alcohol she would wake up her daughter and accuse her of neglect. 'Now that you have a husband and children you only long to forget about me. You would like to see me six foot underground, so that you can inherit my jewellery!'

Angelica knew all too well that she had given Susan an almost pathological dislike of jewellery. Her daughter's clothes had a deliberate down-to-earth dinginess, and Susan only seemed to feel comfortable wearing brown sweaters and worn corduroy trousers. All forms of display and adornment were abhorrent to her. She was devoted to her husband, Michael, who taught English in a private school for boys in Sussex. Susan, herself, ran a successful little kindergarten for pre-school children in her local village. When she spoke about Angelica she usually spoke with a shrugging and maternal tolerance. 'After dealing with Mother, coping with a lot of kids seems like child's play!'

After her behaviour towards her daughter had been

particularly outrageous and taxing, Angelica often started to suffer from remorse. Susan would then suddenly receive a gift package containing several hundreds of pounds worth of jewellery.

'Yet another irritating parcel of Mother's guilt-encrusted pearls and rubies!' Susan would complain to Michael. 'If Angelica would only realise what a bore it is for me to have to spend my whole morning queueing in the post office in order to get her tiresome jewellery back to her.'

Susan very much disliked going up to the city. She saw its pace and petrol fumes as equally threatening and polluting. In the last few months she had felt obliged to make a trip to London once a week, in order to visit Angelica.

'Why do you allow your huge monster of a mother to bully you?' Michael couldn't bear to see the way that Susan could be emotionally manipulated by Angelica. 'She doesn't need to be visited as if she was some kind of terminal invalid. She is far better off than most people. She really lives in rather splendid style on all the loot she has collected from your poor dim wretch of a father. I very much suspect she only ever regarded him as an investment and his death was no doubt quite a bonus for her. You shouldn't allow yourself to be browbeaten by all her hysterical histrionics. I know that she wants us to weep because she has just lost her lover. But I don't see why we all have to accept Angelica's view and treat this very trivial fact as if it was some world-shaking tragedy. Your mother is still quite a formidable and handsome woman and no doubt she will soon find some new and unfortunate fellow. I just wish that I could get it through your head that Angelica is quite all right.'

'I don't think that Mother is all right.' Susan could be very stubborn, as she stood by the stove in her kitchen and fried fish fingers for the children's tea. 'You ought to see the way that she sits there day after day in her throne of a chair in that vast, looming drawing-room with all its ormolu and crystal. I can't stand all those old tapestries and gilded mirrors reflecting other gilded mirrors that she so loves. Mother has always done up all her houses to look like very grand Venetian brothels. And now she is getting older, and now she is alone there is something quite sad about that. Every time I've visited her recently she's been wearing some outrageous and splendid new hair-style and she is dyeing her curls brighter and brighter and her clothes are getting more and more extravagant and magnificent. And the look in her eyes really makes me feel frightened for her. Mother can be very selfish, but she is also quite self-aware and sensitive. Self-obsessed people can suffer just as much as unselfish ones. Mother knows that she is all dressed up with nowhere to go.'

'You mother will survive us all. She has an ego like a bulldozer.'

'I wish I could agree with you. I only pray that her doctor will be of some use to her. I think she is far more vulnerable than you like to imagine. But then I know you have never very much liked her.'

'I like her perfectly well,' Michael would keep insisting. 'I have nothing against Angelica except I find her quite exhausting. I can see that in some ways the old flamingo is really rather a marvellous eccentric personality. But I'll never forgive her for the way she takes advantage of you. . . .'

In the cemetery Angelica moved just in order to keep moving. She felt she was walking with the easy indolence of the very rich when they go shopping. She stopped here. She stopped there. She read some of the epitaphs rather critically. She could have been deliberating whether or not to buy herself a plot.

This evening the whole place appeared to be deserted. The foul weather had apparently discouraged all other visitors. The rain was eating up the light so fast it seemed as if it was already night-time.

On the left side of the graveyard far away in the distance, she saw a shadowy silhouette moving and her heart started pounding. It was that old man – that horrible old fellow that she hated. Yesterday evening he had started following her. Everywhere she went he had pursued her hobbling painfully on his arthritic spindly legs. He had kept a discreet distance, but all the time she had been aware that he was keeping a very strict eye on her. He seemed to be employed as some kind of gardener or caretaker in the cemetery. Before he had decided to supervise all her movements he'd seemed to spend his time pottering around with a broom and sometimes he swept a few leaves off a grave.

She hated the old man because he seemed to find her presence in the cemetery very suspicious. Something in her appearance had made him fear that she was deranged and he also seemed to have detected that her derangement had not been caused by a grief that he could respect. When he followed her she was disturbed by the idea that he felt obliged to do so because he was trying to protect his tombs. He obviously thought that he could expect any kind of obscene and ghoulish behaviour from a stagey-looking woman in a fur coat who loved to wander without good reason in a city graveyard in the rain.

Angelica decided to keep very far away from him. She must never let him know that she had come back here. If he started following her this evening she thought she might very well become hysterical and start screaming at him, 'Get on with your sweeping, you old fucker!' If he hoped to keep his graves free of leaves he had set himself a task that left little time for idling. She felt it would be most unwise of him to provoke her this evening. He would never guess how important it was for her to be allowed to spend some time in this cemetery undisturbed by his hostile spying. If he made her feel persecuted she feared she might become dangerous. She knew she was unwell. She did not feel she was in control. This morning lying in the bath she had felt so demented and raw that she had started to feel sorry for objects. She had cried for her tooth-paste tube because it had lost its top. She had cried for her bath-mat for she had suddenly noticed its sad worn fringe. She had recognised that this was a very bad sign and it had made her think she had better return to the cemetery.

It was when Dr Abelman had suggested she join a bridge club that Angelica had first suddenly had the idea she wanted to visit Brompton Cemetery. His belief that joining any such organisation could help relieve her depression seemed so fatuous that she secretly decided she only wanted to do the opposite of anything that he advised.

Dr Abelman made her feel there was no point in trying to fight her depression, that she might as well try to increase her feeling of gloom by putting herself in the most undesirable situation she could think of. It was then she had thought of the Brompton Cemetery. She had sometimes passed it when she was driving out of London, and she had detested the look of its weird still world where the dead had been scattered, thick as grass seed.

While Dr Abelman went on enthusing about his frightful bridge club, she wondered what would happen if she was to go to that eerie cemetery and sit for a while on some gravestone. Maybe it would be like taking a bath in freezing water in order to feel better once it was over. In the cemetery she would certainly not have any of the 'lively exchanges of ideas' that her insensitive doctor was so keen on, and that seemed something in its favour.

After she left Dr Abelman she had gone home and telephoned Susan. 'I don't think I could possibly feel worse,' she told her. 'I really think something will snap if I go on feeling like this.'

Susan had immediately offered to come up to London and spend the night with her. Angelica said that she couldn't see there would be much use in that. She didn't feel it would help her. She heard a little gasp. She knew she had hurt Susan's feelings. The tone in which she had refused her daughter's offer had been most unpleasant and rejecting. But Angelica felt too savage and discontented to bother to apologise for her ingratitude. She rang off and then she wondered whether she'd told her daughter the truth. Was it really impossible for her to feel any worse? It was then she'd decided she would go off to the Brompton Cemetery and test the truth of her own hectic statement. On her way there in a taxi she had started to feel so frightened she felt she might be playing Russian roulette with her own sanity. She had hated every second she had spent in the graveyard. But when she'd left yesterday evening her relief at getting out had made her feel almost euphoric. Although this feeling had not lasted she was still glad to have experienced it. She knew that no game of bridge was capable of lifting her out of her black moods for even a second.

So she had come back once more to this oppressive place hoping that her fear of being alone with the dead would again drive out all other painful feelings. And already this seemed to be working for she felt light-headed. She had the sensation that she had split in two and part of herself was walking at her own elbow like an over-solicitous nurse endlessly taking the temperature of her own mood. 'You do feel much less wretched since you have been here?' 'Surely it's so abysmal here it can only make you feel better'. 'Surely you are minding much less about Jason now?'

'Oh yes. Oh yes.' Angelica was surprised that she could answer her own over-pampering self so quickly.

'Oh yes. . . .' She already felt very much better. Her terror of the inhabitants of this immense burial ground always acted on her nervous system like an anaesthetic. It numbed all her usual feelings of anxiety and distress. All she could feel was the sickly sweetish sensation of pure fear. The dead continued to terrify her. 'But can it be the dead that I'm frightened of,' she thought, 'surely it really has to be death.' But she still found it seemed to be the dead themselves who petrified her. She couldn't believe she would ever learn to get accustomed to them. She felt she'd forever feel menaced by all the paraphenalia of their grisly crosses, their mausoleums and their elaborate statuary.

'God saw her footsteps falter and he gave his loved one sleep.' Angelica stopped at a grave and she read this epitaph several times. 'Mary Wilkinson 1780–1820.' She could identify very easily with this woman. Angelica thought she knew very well how she must have felt as she faltered. At this moment Mary Wilkinson seemed very much more real to her than Jason. But Angelica was glad to find that she didn't envy this lady and she was glad she was able to walk on and leave her sleeping under her unpleasantly rain-stained stone.

'I am afraid that Jason was a real disaster,' Susan had said to Angelica a few weeks ago. 'I can't bear to see the way he has managed to upset you. And he was such a worthless little creature. I suppose he was quite pretty. But he was never nearly good enough for you. And I'm sure you knew it, Mother. I have to say that I found him an extremely embarrassing figure at all your parties. He dressed up for them much too much. And it used to annoy me to see the way he adored to rush round pouring out drinks for your guests and smiling his awful little "action-man" smile. He never seemed to know how he wanted to be treated. Was he meant to be the son of the house? Or was he the waiter?'

Angelica had looked at her daughter with a certain surprise. Susan was usually so charitable in her attitudes towards other people that it startled her mother to hear her being critical and acerbic. Susan was generally very good-natured and long-suffering when Angelica behaved in an infantile and self-dramatising fashion. She therefore tended to see her as rather blinkered and easily fooled. For this reason it was quite a shock for her to realise that her daughter was quite capable of being sharp and observant and harsh.

Angelica would have liked to pretend that Susan was jealous of her relationship with Jason, but she knew that would be extremely far-fetched. She had to recognise that Jason, with his gold hair and his periwinkle blue eyes and his effete and weak little face, would not have much attraction for her daughter. Jason's idle and exploitative nature could also only arouse Susan's scorn.

Dr Abelman had accused Angelica of bringing out the weakness in Jason's character. 'Your attitude towards this young man was very castrating. You did nothing to help him build up his sense of masculinity. Naturally he resented you for this. You treated him like a pretty trinket. You took no interest in his work.'

Angelica had acted with the hypocritical meekness and compliance that she always chose to show Dr Abelman and she made no protest. However, she had found his accusation quite absurd. When he assessed various situations and made his inevitable errors she never bothered to correct him. She rather enjoyed knowing she was partly to blame for his idiocy because she had fed him false information. She liked sitting there feeling wily as she stared at him with dumbly admiring eyes while he puffed himself up and delivered his silly pronouncements. She could see that he thought he was being very wise and god-like.

Angelica had secretly wondered how this dreary young doctor dared to accuse her of taking too little interest in

Jason's work when from an objective point of view such work had to be considered remarkably uninteresting. When she had first met Jason, he had been running a small boutique which sold kaftans, Eastern straw table-mats, and various kinds of candles, tapers, and oriental beadry. Everything in Jason's shop had been would-be exotic, tawdry and of a very specialised appeal. When he had moved into her house and became her lover, she had urged him to close it. Once his boutique could no longer be regarded as a desperate bid for financial security, she had found it ridiculous for him to spend his days sitting in a stuffy little incense-smelling interior waiting for non-existent customers. Jason had seemed only too relieved when she had encouraged him to get rid of his hopeless little shop. He had given her no hint he found it in any way emasculating.

'Jason seemed to have such a shallow, vain, and greedy personality,' Susan had said to her mother. 'When he used to look at you he always seemed to be looking into your necklace rather than your eyes.'

Angelica had made a weary dismissive gesture with her hand. 'Oh yes,' she said, 'Jason would have certainly loved to find a reflection of himself in my jewellery. You have a very clever point there. But it doesn't help me when you caricature him. I do the same all day long. It never makes me feel any better. I sit here in my house and I tar and feather him with various unpleasant qualities. Sometimes I make him so mean and trite and disgusting that I really overdo it. I then quite defeat my purpose. I endow him with so many nasty traits that I start to feel quite sorry for him. I see him as a poor lost little soul cursed by his own horrible character. That makes him seem very sad indeed. When I start to pity him it's always rather fatal for me. I only wish for one thing then. I only wish to God that he would come back!'

'I don't think that Jason will ever come back.' Susan

had said this to her mother in her most gentle solicitous tones. 'And if you want my frank opinion, I don't think that Jason is the real reason why you now feel so demoralised and blue. You are still a very beautiful and talented woman, Mother. You are someone who once had a brilliant career. I feel convinced that your real trouble is that you have far too much talent and energy to be satisfied leading the lazy life you now lead. It is just not enough for you to sit about in an expensive Chelsea house planning social dinner parties. You were never meant to be a woman who goes to dress-makers and hairdressers. You were not born to spend most of your time lolling around in bed with your pekinese while you gossip on the telephone to other rich and idle ladies. You are simply not fulfilling yourself, Mother. I am certain that is the real reason why you feel so frantic and depressed. I am convinced your doctor would agree with me. I don't believe you will ever be happy until you start working again. The theatre is so exciting nowadays. I never can understand why you don't go back to the stage.'

Angelica had been lying on her huge eighteenth-century four-poster bed during this conversation. She had propped herself up on a mountainous pile of feather pillows and brocaded bolsters. Her head had started to ache while her daughter talked. Susan could sometimes make her feel quite ill, she could be so tactless and bossy.

'Can I just beg something of you, Susan? Can I just implore you on my knees that you never suggest that I take up acting again? If there is any solution for me, the stage is certainly never going to be it. You know how to run nursery schools for toddlers, Susan. I would never presume to give you any advice on that subject. I never want you to dare to speak to me about things which you know nothing about. I can assure you that a stage career is not something which can ever be capriciously resumed once it has been disastrously broken. My career came to an end a very long time ago – I gave up the stage when I first started *you*.'

Angelica had seen the stunned and miserable expression in Susan's eyes. She noticed she had managed to make her daughter blush. She was terrified that Susan was about to suggest she find herself work in television. She therefore didn't care how much she had wounded her. Angelica only wanted her to cut short her visit and leave. If only the girl would have the good sense to get out of her house immediately. If only she would go off and catch a train and get into some smokey compartment and go chugging back to that dull little school-teacher man she had married – start preparing supper for those mousy little thumb-sucking grandchildren.

Angelica could never bear it when Susan brought up her acting. Whenever this happened she could only loathe her daughter for not realising that the whole subject was so disturbing to her that she found it torture to have it mentioned. And because Susan seemed unable to grasp this, Angelica often turned on her with a terrible spite and fury and did her best to punish her. In certain moods Angelica only wanted to make her suffer from a sense of shivering inadequacy. She felt that Susan deserved to be made to feel that her whole existence was worthless because her birth had never been any compensation to her mother for the loss of her stage career.

As Angelica circled round the Brompton Cemetery, she wondered why she kept picking out all the stones and the crosses which had been erected by daughters who mourned their mothers. It offended her to see the way that the modern ones had put up marble monuments which had the slimy texture of plastic. Some of them had even put a nasty little patch of green glass in front of their mother's tombs, so that it lay there like a tiny emerald lawn. It also distressed Angelica to see the way that a lot of the older Victorian mothers were starting to lose their names under the mossy patina of urban dirt which was forming on their stones.

Occasionally, Angelica noticed, there would be a daughter who shared a grave with her mother. She tried to imagine herself sharing with Susan. She found that she always had the same immediate reaction. That would only lead to trouble. She discovered that her imagination was pitifully feeble. She could only ever envisage Susan and herself continuing to retain in death the very same opposing attitudes and qualities that had always grated and clashed in life. Angelica had an image of her own role which filled her with apprehension. She saw herself eternally criticising, exploiting and condescending to Susan. 'I must now be truly insane,' Angelica thought. 'I feel it would be fatal for me to try to share a grave with Susan just as I feel it would be a disaster for both of us if we were to try to share a flat.'

The rain was getting worse. When Angelica stroked her coat it reminded her of the fur of a dog that has just emerged from a pond. She knew she must be frozen to the bone but somehow she couldn't feel it.

'Aren't you frightened you will get pneumonia?' the self that seemed to walk at her elbow asked her. But that self seemed tiresome and over-fussy. She could answer it that she felt fine – that it was a long time since she had felt quite so buoyant and well. As she walked through this jungle of graves a new bounce seemed to have come back into her step and she had the feeling that once again she was suddenly walking like a girl.

She realised there was a very good reason why she felt this unlikely surge of well-being as she walked in this detestable cemetery. She had stopped waiting and that had improved her state of mind far more than Dr Abelman would ever be able to comprehend.

Recently she'd felt that it was waiting that was depleting her physically – that it was this pernicious waiting that was destroying her equilibrium and making her so angry, unbalanced, and melancholy.

She had always found waiting intolerable and recently she had felt she could die of it as she restlessly wandered backwards and forwards from her bedroom, to her bathroom, to the drawing-room, and all the time she had not been able to stop waiting – waiting for Jason to telephone her, waiting for him to write, waiting for him to explain why he'd left without even leaving her a note, waiting for him to tell her that he now realised that he'd made a very great mistake when he left, waiting for the sound of the doorbell that would announce his surprise return.

But in the cemetery she no longer felt she was waiting for anything. Waiting seemed much too futile here. She could imagine that all around her the dead were lying there in the mud and waiting to be alive again. . . .

Angelica deliberately started heading for the very heart of the graveyard where the people who were buried there somehow managed to seem even more dead than the ones who were buried on the sides. She found that if she concentrated she could still just hear the sound of traffic as it rumbled down the Old Brompton Road. But she could only do so by an intense effort of concentration. It was as if the dead had a silence that was so powerful that it could drown out all the ugly and trivial noises of the living.

Angelica started walking much faster as if she had a purpose. She suddenly knew where she was going now. She knew exactly where to find him. Although she had visited him for the first time yesterday evening, she remembered his position very well and she could find her way to Major Arthur Coleman just as easily as if she was one of his sorrowing relations.

As she went hurrying towards him she had the feeling that he was the real reason why she had left the comfort and warmth of her house to make this horrible cold visit to this cemetery.

Once she reached the Major she read again his dates: 'Born 1895 – killed 1917.' It was getting wetter and darker by the moment but she could just make out his fading inscription. 'Life claimed him so he never knew Death.' She found this a little puzzling and for a moment she wondered if there had been an error and the wrong words had been put on his tomb. Maybe someone intended it to read, 'Death claimed him so he never knew Life.' However she had to dismiss this idea very quickly. To make sense of such an epitaph Major Arthur Coleman would have had to have died still-born.

She wondered if he had any descendants who still visited him as he lay lost in this wilderness of grass-bound graves. She felt certain that he had never been married. She found it intolerable to think that he might have ever been married. If anyone now came near him she would only allow it to be a figure that was very remote from him – maybe some grand-niece. But even that was not an appealing idea to Angelica. Dr Abelman had often maintained she had been over-possessive of Jason. But now she found she felt much more over-possessive of Major Arthur Coleman. She wanted to be the *only* person in the world who knew of his existence – more precisely of his non-existence.

He must have been rich, Angelica decided. Or at any rate the young Major's family had been rich enough to buy him an individual stone. She was glad that he had not been jammed into the reserved military acres within this cemetery where 1917 as a year of death seemed just as commonplace as all the identical cheap white crosses that had been issued by the army in much the same way that they provided uniforms.

'I think you can only like men if they are rich,' Jason had once said to her accusingly.

Standing in front of this soldier's grave it seemed a very odd charge to have to answer. But Angelica still wondered if it could be true. Certainly when she tried to give life to the dead young Major she immediately made him financially secure. She would also have to say that Susan's father, Henry, had certainly been very rich. But then if she was to be honest she would have to confess that she had never really liked her late husband. So nothing was to be proved by thinking about him.

She decided that Jason's complaint was only half-true. However, she felt it was interesting to examine why he had made it. She had often found Jason very irritating because he was so spoilt and indolent. He was such a self-applauding young figure that he found it impossible to understand why he often angered her. His mind was very simplistic and he had decided she resented him for not having enough money.

Jason was much too egocentric to be interested in understanding other people's reactions. He had never bothered to observe Angelica very closely. He had never realised that she was like a woman who had been in a car crash many years ago – that she was a person who continued to suffer every day from the results of ancient injuries. He had never quite understood that he was living with someone who had all the rage and malevolence of the cripple. Marriage, motherhood and innumerable love affairs had all disappointed and enraged Angelica. She always found them to be very dull and wretched substitutes for her lost stage career.

It was as if her acting career had been the only heavy vehicle which was capable of carrying the crushing weight of her enormous vanity. She had sometimes had the feeling that her vanity was like a ponderous force that existed almost independent of herself. Far more involved with it than she had ever been with her daughter, Susan, it had always plagued her like a nagging, demanding, child which she never learnt to come to terms with.

Her vanity was incurably restless; it had a desperate need to feel that it was moving. It was insatiably greedy and it longed to feed on the approval of larger and larger audiences.

When her career had crashed, Angelica had never forgiven herself for being the one who was responsible for the accident which had left her vanity permanently confined to a wheel-chair. For many years her whole life had been spent trying to conceal and forget what she felt to be both her crime and her catastrophe. At the age of twenty-nine she had been forced to give up her brilliant stage career, because without obvious reason she had suddenly lost her nerve.

A very similar thing had happened to Angelica's uncle. A rather humourless, fierce man, her uncle had once had a distinguished military career in India. When he had returned to England he had bought himself a house in Sussex and as a child Angelica had often stayed with him. He was an expert horseman and he was the local master of fox hounds. One Saturday he had arrived at the meet as usual. It was a cold day, and the horses snorted dragon-like breath into the frosty air. The horses had whinneyed, and reared, and bucked as they became impatient to get started. Everyone wondered why the hunt never seemed to move off. They wondered why the hounds remained in a huddle, fidgeting and burrowing like worms and baying loudly as the red-coated huntsmen cracked their whips in a frantic effort to control them. Young men and women wearing bowlers, and older ladies in black silk top hats, seated on side-saddles, were forced to jag the mouths of their horses as they became more and more uncontrollable, lashing out with their hooves and biting. They soon started to become angry at the inexplicable delay. Still no-one realised what had happened. A groom went over to help the Master. He assumed he must be having some kind of trouble with his stirrup or his girth. It took the groom, just as it took the rest of the hunt, quite a while to understand what was happening. It took everyone present a long while to believe what they could only find unbelievable. The reason why the hunt never moved off was that the Master had quite suddenly lost the courage to mount.

The poor man had just gone on standing there by the side of his sixteen-hand bay mare. Under his black velvet cap his skin was so pale he looked almost unearthly. As his mare sweated with impatient energy, his forehead also became dotted with perspiration, and his whole face looked measled with shame and anguish. Everyone waited. Everyone went on waiting. Then finally the huntsmen lost their patience. They cracked their whips and the whole hunt moved off and left him.

The following day the hunt committee had a meeting. They decided not to take action for a while. They all assumed that the Master would resign. But he was stubborn. To everyone's dismay he turned up at several subsequent meets and always the same thing happened. He would just stand by his mare and perspire with the same horrible humiliated expression on his face. He once managed to put a foot into his stirrup, but he still never mounted. He just went on hopping foolishly about on the leg which was still unable to leave the ground.

Angelica had often wondered whether her own paralysing loss of nerve had been inherited, whether it ran in her family like a disease that runs in the blood. Or had the dismal example of her uncle made her psychologically prone to the same complaint by undermining her faith that confidence was something to be counted on?

After the hunt had tactfully asked Angelica's uncle to resign he was never the same again. He became so withdrawn and silent that the whole household became frightened of him. He would take long walks, but otherwise he spent most of the day shut away in his study. No-one quite knew what he did in there. Angelica's aunt blamed the hunt for their lack of patience. She cursed them for their ingratitude. She said that they had killed her husband's self-respect, that she doubted he would live very long. She had been right, for he had contracted Parkinson's disease. Angelica had always wondered if it was a ghastly fear of his own inexplicable terror of horses which made his hand shake so much when she watched the way he had to be fed like a baby with a spoon.

Had the sight of her shaking uncle given her a fear of losing courage, which had finally frightened her into the very state of nervous cowardice that she dreaded? Angelica could never decide, although the question still went monotonously round and round in her head like a goldfish in a bowl. She always felt that if she could find the reason for her loss of nerve she might magically recover it. Out of pride she would admit it to no-one, but she had still never lost hope that she might one day be able to act again.

When she was alone at night, she would turn on the television in order to watch the performances of the older actresses. She was always mercilessly critical towards them, feeling that they bungled their roles. But her envy of their national notoriety and the pleasure that they seemed to be taking in their profession would make her feel hot, as if she was running a fever. Angelica would quickly switch off the television, and feel that she had switched off the whole magical world of illusion that she had once loved. Her room seemed immediately dark, even if all the lights were blazing. She would feel that she was like an autumn leaf that had been pressed inside the dark pages of a heavy book. Parchment-crisp, and with every vein still showing, she kept her outline, but her preservation was to no purpose.

Recently she had kept asking herself if Jason had left her

because she was too old. She wondered if he would have minded her being old if she had not given him the feeling that she was something far more oppressive than old – that she was a woman who for a very long time had been dead? Angelica often felt that she was dead in the very same way that she was certain that Jason would also feel himself to be dead once he reached her age. Jason was as vain as she was. He was young and beautiful and for the moment his vanity was still able to feed on the world's response to his boyishness and his beauty. But he was a young man without direction. He was without any specific talents, interests or accomplishments. Angelica often took some vengeful pleasure in prophesying that Jason would feel he was prematurely perishing with his own vanity, once it slowly started to starve to death from the lack of nourishment it was likely to find in middle-age.

Angelica had been playing the lead in a successful drawing-room comedy when her nerve had suddenly left her. One morning she had woken up in a state of white panic. She could remember the name of the theatre where she was expected to appear that evening. She could remember the exact time that the performance started. But, in the night, it was as if certain cells in her brain had been inexplicably damaged, for she found that try as she would, she could not remember the name of the play.

Angelica had found that she could still remember the real-life name of the actor who played opposite her – remember the oily smell of his coarse hair and the feel of his short-fingered hands when for a few weeks he had been her lover. But these memories were so useless they only increased her state of terror, for they in no way helped her to remember any of the lines that she had heard him speaking night after night. If she could just recall some of this actor's lines she kept hoping she might be reminded what the whole play was about. It might help her to know if it was classical or modern. Was it a comedy or was it a tragedy? If she could just remember something about the play, she might suddenly have some memory of the role she had been cast to play in it. She might know if she was meant to be an empress, a suburban housewife or a whore.

Angelica kept having the agonising feeling that she was just about to remember – just about to remember. But then it was as if amnesia had rushed into her brain like water. She had lain in bed and she had cried. She had started shaking so violently that she wondered if she was developing Parkinson's disease like her uncle.

She found that whenever she closed her eyes, she immediately began to see a stage. It was a stage that had no scenery. It had no props to remind her what role she was expected to perform against the blank of its dull, brown back-drop. For a moment she would start to think that she was standing on that stage and while she stood there her brain started filling up with water. Her mind felt it was about to burst; something was filling it up with so much water. She could just make out that down below her there was an audience which was crouching in rows in the dark. The audience was hissing and booing because it knew that there was something wrong with her. It could see that her head had become enormous, that it was swollen with liquid as if she was a victim of hydrocephalus. The audience seemed like a giant mass of evil as it kept screaming and jeering at her. She knew that it was soon going to pelt her with eggs and ice-cream cones. She could feel how much it resented her so for not knowing what part she ought to be playing.

Angelica had managed to get out of bed. She had staggered round her bedroom like a drunkard, trying to find the script of the play. Once she found it and read the title she felt that all the water was suddenly draining out of her brain. She remembered everything. She rang for her maid and told her that she wanted to run through her lines. Her maid gave her a strange look. She had sensed that something in Angelica's manner was very peculiar and it frightened her. When the girl ran through the lines of the play with her and fed her all her cues, Angelica was astonished to find that she was word-perfect. But once she was left alone she immediately telephoned her manager and told him she felt deathly ill and would be unable to appear on stage that evening. It was arranged that her understudy should take over her role. The next day, claiming that her doctors insisted she see specialists, Angelica flew off to Switzerland, where she booked herself in alone at an hotel. She had remained there in hiding for many weeks, feeling unable to get out of bed. Whenever she tried to walk she felt dizzy. She kept having the sensation that she was perched on the parapet of a high turret with a compulsion to jump that struggled against her terror of the hurtling fall.

When she recovered enough to return to England she stubbornly maintained that her illness was physical. She would drop mysterious hints about her rare and dangerous medical condition. She insisted that her doctors had ordered her to have complete rest for many months. She would admit to no-one that she had developed a horror of facing an audience. Some kind of shame made her refuse to admit to the world that ever since her brief seizure of forgetfulness, she lived in perpetual fear that she might once again have the feeling that certain sections of her memory were being swamped as her brain filled up with water. She had no way of telling at what moment this terrifying thing might happen to her. In the theatre they called it 'corpsing'. The very idea of facing any audience had now become enough to make her start shaking. When she thought of trying to resume her career she could only imagine herself as standing there on the stage with a water-logged brain, while her disconcerted fellow-actors stared at her in disbelief and horror as some off-stage prompter was forced to hiss out her entire part.

Very soon after her return to England she startled her friends by her sudden marriage to Henry. Her marriage was a calculated act to salvage what was left of her pride. She became pregnant with Susan and she was able to tell the world that she was unable to take any parts until after the child was born. Henry had admired her for many years. She had always found him a chinless and unexciting young man, and it had bored rather than pleased her that he was mindlessly, uncritically, bedazzled by her. She had never expected nor wanted the marriage to last, but always hoping for the miracle return of her nerve she had felt that she was playing for time. At that moment Henry's enormous wealth had been very valuable to her, for she had been able to use it to camouflage her humiliating failure. It had enabled her to buy outrageously expensive and memorable clothes. She suddenly owned several houses. She had land, valuable possessions, and jewellery. Henry's money had enabled her to live in grand style and it gave her a stage where she could be admired and envied. She entertained lavishly, treating money with contempt, as if she were recklessly scattering it like confetti. She was able to tell the world that the idea of acting now bored her. 'If you are not doing it in order to earn a living – why spend your nights laughing and crying in public in order to get clapped by a lot of vulgar people?'

She became a professional society beauty, and a professional popular hostess. Outwardly she was untiringly flirtatious, and ebullient but inwardly she felt humiliated and stunted, for she felt she had restricted herself to two simple roles when she should have been playing many challenging and world-famous parts.

'It's a bore having you hanging around in London,' she had told Henry. 'You would be far better off improving your out-houses and pottering about your woods with a gun. I think you would be much happier if you spent more time playing the big squire on your estates.'

She was always sneering at him. Whenever he spoke to her she had snubbed him. His vulnerability made her vindictive. She had seen him as having less function than a servant. When he entered a room with his nondescript face, his loose mouth and his baffled, unhappy eyes she wanted to leave it. She told him that he had no humour, and he went off and bought a book of collected jokes, which he tried to read aloud to her in order to disprove her accusation. She became increasingly irritated by his suffering and inarticulate sexual desire for her. Day and night she sensed that he was hoping that she would allow him to sleep with her, although he had long ago lost the courage to try to approach her for he knew that it would make her far too angry. She saw Henry like a gnat, exerting a perpetual pin-prick pressure. She decided that he must be made to live in his house in Somerset. He was puppet-like in the way he made no protest at the plans she made for him. When he moved to the country she sent Susan to live with him there, accompanied by a nurse. Angelica occasionally went down to Somerset to visit them. She considered that the marriage was over, but had no wish for a divorce. She went on living in his house in Chelsea. She had many lovers and kept changing them with great rapidity. She found it impossible to find any man who could keep her interest for very long. Her life lacked challenge, and the act of acquiring a new lover could stimulate her for a little while, but once he had been acquired her interest palled.

But now when she was standing in front of the grave of Major Arthur Coleman she could imagine a relationship with him which would have been very different. 'Life claimed him so he never knew Death.' When she stared at his buoyant, unusual epitaph she felt an anger at the tragedy and the waste of his death. She felt quite certain that she could have loved him, this doomed, young soldier, *bon viveur*. Although he was too claimed by life to ever know death, did he ever have any premonitions how soon it was coming to him?

Born a few years after he had been killed – Angelica saw a cruelty in the mistiming. When she stared at his grave she felt she was starting to see his face hazily emerging from the blank bit of grey stone that lay under his epitaph. He looked very old-fashioned, beautifully glamourised and ethereal with his hair slicked down and his huge eyes dark-shadowed as if he was posing in his uniform for a period photograph.

When Angelica compared Jason to the Major she felt he lacked all panache. He had very little mystery and he was devoid of poignancy. He seemed so inferior to her image of the young and dashing officer that she suddenly found it almost impossible to understand how she had ever allowed herself to become so unhappily obsessed by him. Arthur Coleman made Jason seem cheap and modern and unappealing. He had none of the gallantry and the romance of the fallen soldier. Arthur Coleman reduced Jason and made him seem ordinary. He turned him into a dreary little creature who belonged with the unexciting crowds of youngish people with fume-stained and impoverished faces who swarmed the dirty London streets wearing shoddy and self-conscious clothing.

Angelica found that, curiously enough, it was Jason whom she felt she had invented as she stood like a grief-stricken fiancée looking down at the tomb of the lost Arthur. She saw this First World War casualty and herself as well-matched. They'd both been fatally crippled by wounds acquired in another era.

If Arthur Coleman were to suddenly rise up from the ground Angelica had no feeling that it would frighten her. She believed she would embrace him. She saw this soldier as having served his purpose just as he had served his country. He had done what Dr Abelman had so singularly failed to do. He had killed her self-destructive obsession with Jason.

She could see the ease with which she had been able to conjure up an attractive and lovable Major. She had only needed to keep her eyes fixed on his death date. She saw that she could make herself feel a real sense of loss and sorrow when she thought of all the dances she would never be able to have with this phantom. She saw how she could nearly make herself cry when she thought of all the wine and the kisses and the jokes she would never be able to share with him. And when she recognised how much passion she would have liked to have poured out on Major Coleman it made her have complete distrust for her old feelings for Jason.

Angelica knew that she could go home now. Jason had lost all his power to make her wish to hide from the world behind the prison-like arched railings of this cemetery. All her interest in him had died so suddenly that he now seemed far more dead than the Major. If she was to return to her house and find that he had decided to come back to her, that he was there, wearing fancy patched jeans and sprawling on the sofa of her drawing-room, she felt she might easily start to scream as if she had seen some ghastly resurrected apparition. It was the everyday Jason that she dreaded she might find drinking her whisky with a shifty, disarming, little-boy smile.

When she thought about him as she was standing in the Brompton Cemetery, she found her images all came from her surroundings. It seemed to her that when he had left her with such aggressive abruptness, her memory had buried the unsatisfactory, everyday Jason and replaced him with a glorified statue. But now the original figure of her young lover was rising up again and smashing the romantic statue she had erected in his honour. She remembered the grey and annoying soles of his bare feet as he sat around all day on the carpet of her drawing-room, with his blond John-the-Baptist hair dripping down over the pop records that he liked to play so repetitively on her stereo.

'What have you arranged for us to do today?' He always used to keep asking. 'What have you arranged?' Most of the time he seemed to be bored as a lonely child on a dull Sunday afternoon.

'I have arranged for us to commit double suicide,' she would snap at him. She was always infuriated by this question for it made her realise she felt far too tired to have the energy to spend her days amusing him.

Angelica felt quite free to leave now. She had come creeping into this cemetery, a woman with jangling nerves, who felt imprisoned by a sense of bitterness and defeat. But now she believed she could leave with the confidence and freedom of someone who had made an important decision. She would go home. She would go back to all the ordinary routines of her life, and she would secretly go on loving the Major.

Everything was shadowy and misted in the rainy twilight of this cemetery, and her own thoughts seemed to be the only things which were bright and clear. If she wanted to go on loving an elusive phantom, she now saw it as lunacy not to go on loving the Major. The rasping reality of his presence would never be able to tarnish his golden, gallant image. Arthur Coleman would never be able to give her any chafing memories. She could be quite certain that her vanity would be safe just as long as she saw that her affections remained cautiously focused on his invisible soldier's body. The Major would most certainly never tell her that he only really liked sleeping with people who were as beautiful as himself.

Even in this graveyard Angelica could still hear Jason whispering these words so gently. He had been lying beside her in her large billowy bed. He had sounded very affectionate as if he was sleepily and sweetly musing aloud. She had not answered, stretched out beside him. She had felt lifeless and stiff as a chloroformed patient being wheeled from the operating table. She had never expected that Jason's narcissism would turn on her and stab her. It had always amused her to flatter him. She had loved to keep praising his physical beauty. She had assumed that he would always be pleased by the way she was prepared to share his obsessional pride in his own beauty, for she could believe that she herself still had beauty – while she still had him.

Now that Angelica could see that all her romantic feelings for Jason might just as well be transferred to the Major, she felt she was able to step back and stare at her old relationship in much the same detached and critical way that she liked to stare at the names which were engraved on the various gravestones in this cemetery. She could admit that she had underrated Jason when she assumed that he would find her attitude towards him so flattering as to be forever satisfactory. She could understand that he might well have felt threatened by something covetous and greedy in the way she had loved to keep kissing and praising his body. Had he started to see her as an aged thief who was trying to appropriate for herself the only valuable asset he believed himself to possess?

Jason had always had indolent, amateurish, theatrical ambitions. He believed that with his good looks he could very easily become a popular television idol. He had hoped naively that she would help him make contacts with producers and directors. He had never been able to understand why she had so little interest in helping him to 'get spotted'. Jason had always seen her as an actress from such a hopelessly bygone era that it never occurred to him that she herself nursed unrealistic ambitions, had secret fantasies in which she recovered her nerve and made a sensational theatrical 'come back'.

When she had made no effort to help him make useful film contacts Jason had started to distrust her and he had slowly grown to loathe her. Just as she had seen little future for herself in promoting a theatrical career which was not her own, so Jason had seen little point in continuing to be the lover of an older woman, who threw jealous dramatic tantrums, and only wanted to use his beauty like a raft to keep her own vanity afloat as it passed through the choppy seas of middle-age.

Angelica suddenly had the feeling she was acting. Thoughts kept rushing through her brain, and it was as if she was acting them, rather than thinking them. She had the curious sensation that she was performing for the Major, that he was her captive and unresponsive audience. She knew her role was not particularly engaging, but that didn't seem to have much significance. All that now seemed important was that she should realise, once and for all, that this must be her last act.

When Jason had left her he had taken away any sense that she was still attractive and that her life still had potential. She could see now that it was the theft of this feeling rather than the loss of this shiftless and bored young man which had brought about her collapse. When she had wanted him back it was as if she was hoping that he would bring her back this valuable feeling, as a conscience-stricken thief might return a stolen purse. This feeling would not have been so vital to her if she had not needed it to prop up the rickety fabric of her fantasy that she would one day make a successful theatrical comeback. When she left the Brompton Cemetery Angelica was now convinced that it was this deadly pipe-dream that must be left behind with the Major.

Angelica decided that she would telephone Susan when she got back home and she'd tell her the truth about her stage career. She would try to unpick all the boastful, defensive lies that she had told her daughter throughout the years and admit that it was cowardice rather than marriage and motherhood that had brought her career to such an abrupt full-stop. She'd explain how she'd developed such a terror that she might 'corpse' on stage that she had to decide she could no longer act. She would tell Susan that she now wondered whether her seizure of stage panic had been as neurotic and unmotivated as her vanity had always liked to imagine. Was there not always the possibility that her fear of making an appearance had been perfectly valid and she had used stage-fright as a cover-up for her own incompetence? Maybe she had been frightened to test whether the success of her youthful stage appearances were due to her beauty rather than to any real gifts as an actress. By retiring so young had she not evaded all trial of her talent and allowed herself the luxury of a lifetime spent mourning the tragic waste of abilities which very probably existed only in the fancies of her own mind?

Angelica wondered why she had such a need to confess all this to Susan. She had never told Dr Abelman that she'd ever had an acting career at all. She couldn't bear him to know about its ignominious ending. She was frightened that if he knew he would have many views on the subject and they would be simplistic and censorious and she felt it would be insufferable to have to listen to them.

As his approach to all problems was very heavy-footed he would probably make some irritatingly useless suggestion. He might well urge her to join some amateur theatrical group – the kind of untalented group that tours all the prisons in England putting on embarrassing productions of Shakespeare for the hapless inmates.

But with Susan she was finally going to be honest, so that something beneficial would be gained from her eccentric visits to the cemetery. She was certain that her daughter would treat this attack on herself as just one more histrionic declaration. 'We all get moods like these, Mother,' Susan would very likely say with her usual patient, school-teacher briskness. 'Remember, they always pass. You should try to take more care of yourself – maybe cut down on the whisky – see that you get more rest.' Angelica knew that Susan would never be able to believe that she was speaking seriously. Since her earliest childhood Susan had been brought up to accept without question her mother's version of her own life, and by now she would find it more painful than Angelica had if she was suddenly forced to revise it.

She re-read the Major's epitaph as if it was a courteous way of saying goodbye to him and started slowly walking back towards the entrance of the cemetery. She noticed that two figures were coming in. In the distance she could just make out that they were a man and a woman, and the man seemed to be pushing something that looked like a wheel-barrow.

For a moment Angelica felt an unreasonable surge of resentment and antagonism, as if the Brompton Cemetery had become her own private terrain and the new couple were trespassers. Then her attitude changed and she decided that she would like to speak to them. Normally it never occurred to her to wish to speak to strangers. But after the lonely one-sided dialogue that she had been carrying on with the Major, the idea that this couple could listen and respond made them seem very attractive.

She felt certain that they would be quite glad to talk to her. They too must be suffering from a feeling of chill and panic as they walked through the chaos of graves in the rain. In these stark unusual surroundings she believed she would be able to speak to this couple in a more honest and intimate way than she had ever been able to speak to her husband, her daughter, her lovers or any of her friends.

She saw they were heading for a clump of evergreens that lay upon the far left side and Angelica started to follow them. There was something very purposeful in the brisk way they were walking without speaking. They seemed to know their way through all the complicated, twisting paths, and she felt they had visited the Brompton Cemetery many times before.

The couple suddenly stopped, and as Angelica came nearer to them she saw that it was a pram that the man had been pushing and that it was loaded with potted geraniums. The woman was kneeling down in the wet grass beside a mound without a stone. She had a trowel in her hand and was ripping out all the dead flowers that had been planted on this newly dug patch of earth. She kept tossing them over her shoulder with a frenetic violence. She then very gently replaced them with the geraniums which she took from her battered and paint-chipped pram.

Angelica stood at a distance and hesitated before approaching her. She felt suddenly intimidated by the way the woman seemed to be totally absorbed in trying to plant the geraniums so closely together that they spread over the mound in a solid quilt of red. The man was standing a few yards away from the woman and his back was turned to her. He looked as if he was keeping guard. Angelica saw that he was about thirty-five, that he was not good-looking. He was wearing a shabby rain-coat. The expression on his face was both embarrassed and grim. Something about the way he was just standing there with his arms crossed made Angelica feel that he must have stood and waited while the woman planted her flowers many times before. After hesitating, Angelica decided that she would walk past the woman and she would smile at her. She hoped she would realise that this was not a meaningless social gesture. It was with the woman that Angelica now felt that she would like to establish an intimate relationship. The man she found a little unprepossessing. She felt there was something rather gloomy in the way he just stood there like a sailor on deck staring out over the sea-like grey wash of tombstones.

Angelica suddenly had the feeling that the woman would not find her deranged if she tried to explain how she had cured her depression by using the grey stone of the Major as if it was a sounding-board.

She suddenly longed to tell someone that she felt happier than she had felt for years. She felt futureless, but that very feeling now gave her a perverse sense of freedom. When she left and went out of the gates into the Old Brompton Road, she would know she was not going anywhere in particular. Coming out of the colourless enclosures of the cemetery she would be glad just to blink like a blinded mole, unaccustomed to the vulgar flash of advertisements and lights in all the shops. The usual crowds with their plastic rain-coats and umbrellas would be jostling along the pavements if she was to walk down the Earls Court Road. Having no direction, she would be glad to let them push her along wherever they were going.

If some odour of the cemetery was still clinging to her damp fur coat no-one would notice it in this street, where seedy Oriental restaurants expelled a steam of cheap sour fat smells from all their cellars. She would attract very little attention as she was sucked along in the current of the evening rush-hour, one more woman with bitter, exhausted eyes, whose beauty was now something that was clumsily stencilled on the corrugated surface of her face with make-up aids. If she did not stand out in the crowd, it would not trouble her. She would be much too glad to feel that she could still be part of it. She would be happy just because she was no longer in the Brompton Cemetery with its haphazard stones that insisted on nothing except losses from the past – happy just to forget the way that the cemetery seemed to offer her nothing except its own dismal future. While she was with the crowd that breathed, and hurried, and sweated, she would feel exuberant like a schoolgirl on holiday. She would find it intoxicating to escape from the cemetery's sombre insistence that there was nothing but the past and the future, and she would skim along the wet pavements as part of the crowd that she would love for making her feel she could still be part of the present.

Angelica was certain that the kneeling woman would understand her new mood. If the woman responded to her smile, she decided that she would invite the couple to come back home with her. She felt a great sympathy and liking for the woman. It was very possible that she was also trying to come to terms with a festering sense of general failure. Maybe she was trying to speak to herself through the medium of that geranium-dotted mound, just as she had tried to speak to herself by making use of the grave of the Major.

Angelica started walking down the path that led past the spot where the woman was kneeling. When she got close to her she smiled. The woman looked up from her planting. Her distraught eyes stared at Angelica. They seemed not to see her at all.

Angelica walked quickly on. She felt that something was pressing inside her chest, interfering with her breathing. The woman's snub was registering on her very slowly. She could remember every detail of the woman's face. She could still see the way the rain had turned her hair into a dark paste that smeared her forehead. She remembered the shine on the knobs of the woman's angular protruding cheekbones, her over-long upper lip, the anguished expression in her cavernous, exhausted eyes. Angelica was used to attracting a lot of attention wherever she went with her still handsome face, her exaggerated halo of bright golden curls, her make-up which was applied as thickly as grease-paint, her general air of hectic and arrogant authority. It shocked her to realise that the woman had chosen to notice nothing about her at all.

Angelica suddenly wished that she could run. She cursed her weak ankles. She longed to run out of the iron gates and into the streets. The strange woman had ruined the Brompton Cemetery.

Angelica knew that she could never again come back. She realised that she would have many lonely evenings in the future. She would have moods of panic and black depression and she'd drink whisky until she felt that the alcohol was burning a passage through the centre of her brain. She'd often get extremely drunk, and extremely maudlin and poor Susan would have to listen to the scream of her melodramatic ravings. But however dark her moods might become she knew she would never come back to the cemetery.

Angelica was convinced that the woman had refused to acknowledge her smile because she saw her very presence in this cemetery as an obscenity. Her unseeing stare had made Angelica feel like a criminal. She felt accused by the sorrow in the eyes of that woman, just as yesterday she'd felt accused by the antagonistic looks of the decrepit old caretaker.

She was certain that the woman with the gaunt cheekbones had not come to soak for a while in the melancholy atmosphere of this graveyard, hoping that when she left she would feel more grateful for life than when she had arrived. She had not come here to hover neurotically round the grave of an unknown soldier hoping she could derive some tiny sense of her own vitality by devoting herself to the grey slab that symbolised his deadness. When that woman had come through the black iron gates of the cemetery with her pram-load of geraniums she had not come trundling in with a load of selfish depressive anxieties that she was asking these weed-strewn inmates to dispel.

Angelica shivered. The kneeling woman had made her feel trite and despicable. It suddenly occurred to her that even if Jason was buried here in this cemetery it would not be right for her to come to visit him. If he had a place here she might be able to view him with less resentment and bitterness. It was possible she then might be able to endow him with a few of the heroic qualities she had found so pleasant to ascribe to the Major.

But even if she was to come to Jason's grave and was to stand beside it with her head bowed while she strewed it with some of the feelings of sadness and regret that she'd been able to whip up for the long-dead officer, she realised that her emotions would still have no validity since she would always be acting them rather than feeling them.

Angelica saw herself as a creature so pathetically in need of an audience that even if she was to come as a mourner to this vast metropolitan graveyard, there would always be a part of herself that stood back so that it could play the role of the applauding audience to the sensitivity of her own feelings.

She knew that she would most certainly never return. The woman with the geraniums had made her feel too ashamed. She knew that woman had not come here to play-act. She had not come here to stalk about among the graves as if she was striding the boards. Angelica could see by the sorrow on that stricken woman's face that she had lost someone she loved.

Angelica had created a great storm about her losses, but confronted by this grieving couple she recognised them to be very trivial losses indeed. If she could be made to feel more self-disgust within the cemetery than she often felt in the world outside its railings, she knew that nothing could induce her to make another visit.

As Angelica walked out into the Old Brompton Road, the lights of the passing cars seemed unkind and over-bright and searching. They in no way seemed pleasant to her just because their glare was strange after the greyness of the cemetery. There were people with umbrellas walking the pavements. They were breathing, smiling, talking, but that in no way made them seem attractive. She had hoped that after the loneliness of the time she had spent amongst the tombstones, it would be elating to feel she could belong with them. But she looked at them all with disgust, seeing only faults in their complexions, their bodies and their clothing. She was once again all too aware of their ears and she found the idea of trying to belong with them intensely unappealing.

As she went out of the gates she felt like an outcast. She suddenly loathed the woman with the geraniums for driving her back into the world. She detested her for making her feel there was something repulsive in coming to visit the Major.

She started wandering slowly up towards the Earls Court Road. She noticed that the wet pavements outside all the houses and restaurants were littered with the most repulsive conglomeration of aggressively uncollected rubbish. There must be a strike. And even if the strike was to one day end, Angelica was certain that it must be far too late, for the rubbish had been allowed to pile so high she could hardly believe that it was now possible for anyone ever to collect it.

She realised that she had not got rid of the dark cruel vision that came from her paranoia. She had not found calm or acceptance from visiting the peaceful non-striving world of the buried. She was tortured by the feeling that she had put on some kind of ghastly performance within the cemetery and it had made her a laughing stock. She had presented some part of her life and it had provided a very shaming spectacle.

Now Angelica felt the consuming fury of the disgraced performer – a murderous loathing of the audience who had failed to appreciate the display she had put on for them. But she also recognised that it was insane when she tried to blame the dead for their lack of enthusiasm for the shoddy little show she had just enacted in their midst. All her anger had to be transferred therefore to the living, for she suspected she would have no more success if she was to perform in front of a live audience than she'd had with the vast deaf multitudes of the deceased.

When she reached the Earls Court Road, Angelica stood on a corner, and with a wicked and baleful eye she watched the crowds as they went streaming by her. So many Arabs and Indians and Africans passed her she could hardly believe she was in London. She disliked the look of all of them, finding them alien, but not in the least exotic. She saw them as having very dark ears under their turbans and their romantic flowing head-dresses.

Her attitude to the English people who hurried past was equally ungenerous. She assessed them with the same coldness that she'd always assessed the people she had allowed to stream like strangers through her life.

She saw various unexciting-looking young matrons and they seemed very like Susan. They were pushing small children in prams and strollers. Most of the kids that these young women had produced seemed truly awful to Angelica. Her attention deliberately focused on the ones who were either bawling or whining. She saw them as sticky and smelly and unrewarding, and she couldn't believe their mothers really liked them.

It quite pleased her to see that many of these young women looked tired and harassed, for she could feel no pity for them. In her opinion, they had been idiotic and lazy and they'd settled for a life of the most horrible domestic routine and drudgery in order to give birth to more mindless and ugly human specimens who would lead much the same lives that they had.

When she examined the young men who were going by her, she soon picked out the ones who could remind her of Jason. Some of them seemed to be even vainer than he was, and they took more care with their appearance. She noticed one or two who were much more beautiful than he had ever been. They were taller and better built and their faces were stronger and more intelligent. She would have liked to have pointed them out to Jason and she cared very little if this desire was spiteful and unworthy.

It gave her a malignant pleasure to imagine a discerning and powerful film director who was looking for a glamorous male to cast as the juvenile lead in an important movie. If languid little Jason was to try for the part, she was certain he would never be able to compete with the handsome figures she could discover in the streets. But although she was relieved that it was so easy to find young men who were much more attractive than he was, she was glad she didn't envy any of the girls who were walking arm-in-arm with them. For surveying the crowds like a street prostitute on the look-out for clients, Angelica's vision was so bitter she could only see every man that passed as the bearer of a couple of sickening ears.

For a moment she stared downwards at the rain-water that was trickling sluggishly in the gutter. She noticed that it had a thick top scum of oil from all the vehicles which were jamming, and hooting, and blowing hot foul air from their exhausts as they headed down to the river. She wondered if these oily rainbow colours had a modern beauty. If they did, she knew she was never going to learn to like it. The gutter water was heading for a drain, and she saw the Earl's Court crowds as hurrying towards a very drain-like future.

Angelica tried to imagine what would happen if she was suddenly to start to sing a song as she stood there on the corner? What would happen if she was to start to do a little dance? She assumed that all the young men would laugh and nudge their girls as they pointed out a poor buffoon of a woman who was making an exhibition of herself on a busy street.

If she began to sing and dance she imagined that one or two old ladies with respectable hats and handbags would frown and purse their lips as they went limping along the pavements on painful swollen legs. They might think of reporting her to a policeman, but if they decided she looked quite harmless, they would not bother to waste their time and they would shuffle off and leave her. A certain amount of unshaven men with eyes that looked like bleeding pools of alcohol would be bound to stumble past her as they went from pub to pub, as if they could never abandon their quest for the perfect drinking bar. They would stare at her with a glazed incuriosity, seeing a noisy woman whirling in her fur coat in the rain, and they'd go staggering on. As they drifted past her in their habitual state of topsy-turvy unreality she would never be able to startle them, although they might well mistake her for an escaped circus dancing bear.

Angelica could hardly believe that all the homosexuals who were hanging around waiting for assignments would be all that impressed by her performance either. The stern and sadistic boys dressed in black leather, the ones with the fierce compressed lips who wore studs and swastika arm-bands in much the same way that she wore jewellery, they would simply all ignore her. The boys who looked just as flamboyant and feminine as she did might feel more threatened by her extrovert display, and they would quickly cross to the other side of the street.

But she wondered what would happen if all these crowds were suddenly to stop and gather round her? What would happen if they all decided to postpone all their important engagements and chose just to stand around enraptured listening to her song and applauding her while she danced? If they reacted with no embarrassment seeing a crazed woman performing her sad and drunken antics on a rainy urban corner – if, on the contrary, by some inexplicable miracle, they adored her performance – if they encouraged more and more people to gather round her – if they all roared encouragement as they begged her to continue, Angelica wondered if she would still see all these people as quite so sordid, dull, and doomed.

But she knew that she was never going to dare to perform for the crowds. She knew she must never forget the only valuable lesson she had learnt in the cemetery. She must forever abandon the destructive fantasy that she was ever going to act in public again.

As she went on looking at the driven, ugly faces of the people who were streaming past her, she felt a savage resentment as she remembered the lady with the geraniums. Angelica suddenly longed to be back alone with the dead, back alone with her heroic imaginary Major. But she started waving for a taxi that would take her back to the comforts of her home.